PESTILENCE IN ABYSSINIA

A NOVELLA

STEPHEN A. KLOTZ

Copyright © 2021 Stephen A. Klotz

All rights reserved. No part of this book may be reproduced, stored, or transmitted by any means—whether auditory, graphic, mechanical, or electronic—without written permission of both publisher and author, except in the case of brief excerpts used in critical articles and reviews. Unauthorized reproduction of any part of this work is illegal and is punishable by law.

ISBN: 978-1-957203-08-9 (sc)
ISBN: 978-1-957203-09-6 (hc)
ISBN: 978-1-957203-10-2 (e)

Because of the dynamic nature of the Internet, any web addresses or links contained in this book may have changed since publication and may no longer be valid. The views expressed in this work are solely those of the author and do not necessarily reflect the views of the publisher, and the publisher hereby disclaims any responsibility for them.

The Ewings Publishing LLC
One Galleria Blvd., Suite 1900, Metairie, LA 70001
1-888-421-2397

The sides of the mountains were covered with trees, the banks of the brooks were diversified with flowers; every blast shook spices from the rocks, and every month dropped fruits upon the ground. All animals that bite the grass or browse the shrubs, whether wild or tame, wandered in this extensive circuit, secured from beasts of prey by the mountains which confined them.

—*Rasselas. Prince of Abyssinia*
by Samuel Johnson

CONTENTS

FLIGHT TO ADDIS

Robert Caanen boarded a plane at Dulles Airport for the first leg of a fourteen-hour trip to Addis Ababa. On the way, he engaged in sporadic chitchat with a fellow passenger, a retired airline pilot with a Scandinavian accent. He and his American wife were traveling to Istanbul with friends.

"What do you want to do this thing for in Ethiopia?" the man asked. "I flew to Addis several times. It's really poor."

"Yes?" Caanen said.

"Sounds like a crazy plan to me," the former pilot said. "I'd rather spend my time somewhere beautiful. That is not Addis. No! And it is near the Sudan."

The State Department had recently issued a warning to US citizens to avoid the Sudan. The situation in Darfur was worsening, and the safety of foreigners could not be guaranteed.

Caanen was a member of a small international contingent of physicians sent to help Ethiopians initiate antiretroviral drugs for the treatment of AIDS. He removed a paperback book from his shoulder bag. He was looking forward to an uninterrupted reading of Döblin's *Berlin Alexanderplatz* with its rich cast of down-and-out Berliners. It was entertaining reading while still in the West, but several weeks later, having moved into his temporary cubicle in Ethiopia, he laid down the book, only partially read, not to be opened again. The description of European culture and the book's flow of consciousness were too incongruous for someone living in the Ethiopian Highlands. This was a theme he would return to frequently while living there. He felt his principles were out of synchrony with what occurred in Ethiopia.

Caanen struggled to get comfortable in a nonaisle seat for the next eight hours. He was more than six feet tall, with a barely perceptible midriff bulge that he was at pains to minimize. He had light-brown, curly hair tinged with gray above the ears, and at sixty-three years of age, he was often mistaken for someone ten to fifteen years his junior, a fact that no longer amused him. He was twice divorced and often lonely, as his three children busily made their own lives.

After landing in Frankfurt, all the male passengers hurriedly deplaned and bolted for the small water closets scattered around the international concourse. Caanen waited in line for a toilet with Indian men returning to New Delhi. Most of them had just completed a *locum tenens* in Los Angeles or Chicago with computer software companies.

The last leg of the trip to Addis was in a half-filled plane. The next stop, however, was not on the itinerary. Suddenly, they were on course for Khartoum. The flight path paralleled the Nile. The river glinted with sparks of light in the darkling sunset. It was flooding, inundating orchards and plowed lands. The uniform ochre of the ground was broken only by shimmering light from weak incandescent bulbs on the sides of buildings. As the plane approached Khartoum, Caanen saw minarets towering above all other structures. They were so numerous they appeared to be only yards apart.

After landing in Khartoum, American and European passengers deplaned wearing ball caps, T-shirts, and blue jeans while pulling wheeled aluminum suitcases. They arrived in Khartoum as if returning home, opening their cell phones and making local calls while dragging their luggage down the aisle. The plane stopped more than for an hour and refueled.

The remaining few passengers flew on to Addis Ababa where it was pitch-dark. The city was enshrouded in a thunderstorm. Caanen peered out the window at the streaking rain on the glass. Individual raindrops were visible, highlighted by the flashing shaft of red light from the tip of the wing.

Caanen went through customs and out into the airport foyer looking for his contact. A young Ethiopian woman held up a sheet of paper with "Canine" scrawled on it in black marker. He gestured with his arm toward the woman who then led him to a taxi. The taxi driver, wearing casual clothes, leaped out from the front seat, opened the trunk, and tossed in Caanen's bags.

"I'm Testfaye," the driver said. "I take you to your 'otel." He smiled broadly, showing his white teeth.

Caanen sat down on the passenger side of the front seat. He would come to know these beat-up Toyota taxis intimately. Testfaye's ID card was displayed on the visor above the driver's seat. A cheap green textile coverlet with red tassels lay on the dashboard. All the taxis had manual shifts, were at least ten years old, and could barely negotiate the slightest incline. The drivers must have attended the same driving school, where the main objective was to put the vehicle into the highest gear as soon as possible. Consequently, taxis lugged about in third and fourth gear, and the passengers lurched about in their seats.

The roads in Addis were abominable, but Testfaye knew the location of every pothole and veered sharply to avoid striking them head-on. Caanen attempted to look at the buildings along the streets as Testfaye drove along Bole Road from the airport to the hotel. He could only see sheets of corrugated tin forming barricades at the curbside. There was an occasional building undergoing construction visible above the fencing. Water rushing across intersections and sluicing into the ditches fell under the glare of the headlights. The torrents had a red-brown tinge.

"Here you are, sir. 'otel Leopol. I pick you up at nine tomorrow and take you to headquarters."

After bidding Testfaye good night, Caanen stood in the dark at the hotel entrance in a light shower. Preserved under glass at each side of the entrance were a black-maned lion to the right and a leopard to the left. The animals were obviously mounted by a novice taxidermist. Their limbs were globular, like a child's doll. The eyes were mounted at a bias, giving the animals a cross-eyed look. Moreover, the glass eyes had lost their luster.

Caanen entered the hotel foyer, which was lit with forty-watt incandescent bulbs. He stopped and released his luggage and looked up at a tall, lithe receptionist behind the counter, dressed in a magenta skirt and jacket with gold piping on the cuffs and collar and a flight cap on her head. She handed the room key to Caanen without a word of greeting.

He took the elevator to the seventh floor and entered his room. He opened the French doors to the balcony and looked out over the damp city with its streetlights shining on Jomo Kenyatta Boulevard. An Ethiopian Orthodox church a block away blared a message to the faithful from a loudspeaker in *Ge'ez*, the ancient language of the country, now used only in church services. The racket went on past midnight and was interspersed with pounding drum music.

Caanen carefully inspected a twenty-five-gallon metal drum fastened to the ceiling of the shower cubicle—the water heater. Naked copper wiring dangled below the showerhead. The heater had to be turned on at night in order for the water to run hot in the morning. A memory of Thomas Merton stepping out of his shower in Thailand, plugging in a fan, and dying of electrocution came to Caanen's mind.

The night was cold. There was no heat in the hotel. Caanen awoke in the early-morning hours to a chorus of baying dogs, numbering perhaps in the hundreds, after a police siren sounded. Near daybreak, he lurched awake one more time when the muezzin of a neighboring mosque called the faithful to prayer.

THE DUTTON FOUNDATION

"**M**orning, Testfaye. Where are we going?" Caanen asked. "We go to headquarters of Dutton Foundation. Big NGO. My boss." Testfaye smiled.

There were scattered clouds in the sky, the sun was refulgent, and the street surfaces were drying rapidly. The humidity was barely perceptible. A pair of black kites wheeled and swooped at one another, slowly passing out of sight behind the hotel.

Caanen had travelled to many foreign countries but, none quite like this. He grinned at the thought of being in Ethiopia, the ancient Abyssinia. Samuel Johnson had written a text about Abyssinia, a short book about happiness and how one finds it. Caanen pondered whether he would be happy in this home of Haile Selassie and the Rastafarians?

Testfaye drove the taxi in lurching movements several blocks to the Dutton lot. A large metal sign stood before the building, its edges warped. Rust seeped onto the two-foot-tall chrome lettering spelling out: DUTTON. Here was the Non-governmental organization or NGO Testfaye had spoken of.

Testfaye's cell phone rang. "Hello, Mr. Peter. We here now." Testfaye turned to Caanen and gestured toward the front door.

A large, solid fellow in his midtwenties came to the entrance. The doorman swung the glass door outward and stepped aside.

Peter Evers pushed out a plump hand toward Caanen. "Welcome aboard, Dr. Caanen. Come on up. We'll have a short meeting and presentation about the foundation."

The two took the elevator to an upper floor and entered an office suite with "Dutton Foundation" printed on a sheet of paper taped to the door. There were two columns of desks in the elongated room, and each desk lined up closely behind the other. One column was empty, and the other was occupied with neatly dressed young men and women staring at computers on their desktops. The oldest member was introduced to Caanen as the associate director of the country for health planning.

"This is Tim. He is our oldest hand on the staff," said Evers.

Tim, a man in his early forties with thinning blond hair, was wearing a blue silk tie and white dress shirt. "Glad to meet ya, Doc," Tim said as he shifted his eyes away from his computer and looked up.

The other workers did not look up.

After the perfunctory greeting, Caanen and Evers entered the boardroom where the windows were thrown wide open. Hammering and shouting could be heard outside. A new high-rise building was going up in an adjacent lot.

Evers was wearing a sage green jacket over a gray sweater, black slacks, and brightly polished brown penny loafers. He sat with his legs crossed and pumped his left leg as he spoke.

"Excuse me a moment," he shouted into the office. "Have them deliver two macchiatos!" He then reached for his cell phone. "Testfaye. I left my wallet somewhere in my bedroom. Can you find it for me and bring it to the office?"

After directing Testfaye, Evers turned his attention toward Caanen.

"Well, first, you need to know that Dutton takes a personal interest in Ethiopia. Dutton himself was just here several weeks ago meeting with the president of Ethiopia. No one in the world has the star power he has. When he was president of the United States, he met most of the African leaders. He told me that the present leadership of Ethiopia is good. I don't see it myself," Evers said as he leaned over and opened his laptop.

Evers gave a summary of the HIV epidemic in Ethiopia and some preliminary statistics about the area Caanen was assigned to. It was a thirty-minute PowerPoint presentation. At the end of every sentence, his voice rose and was accompanied by a wagging gesture with his right index finger. The clinic that Caanen was assigned to had already enrolled more than three thousand patients. The vast majority of them were from rural areas without electricity, water, or an address. Caanen learned that he was to go to Dessie, a city northeast of Addis. It was only two hundred miles by road, but nine hours of driving due to the appalling road conditions. Dessie was a provincial capital, a *woreda* or district of Wollo Province. It had a storied past in Ethiopia's history.

"Let's drink our macchiatos," Evers said, leaning back in his chair. "You know the great thing about the Foundation is that we're young and bright, and we bring a lot of enthusiasm to the job—twice what you'd get with older workers. Being the deputy country director, I've got my finger on what we've accomplished, and it's incredible. I don't know what you know about the NGOs here, but we are the premier organization. The other NGOs don't quite have the intellectual capital we have." Evers paused, looked at his cell phone, and continued talking. "Normally I don't give this presentation—it's not my kind of thing—but our placement director is in Lalibela for the weekend on holiday."

Evers changed topics. "You know, I just met with a consultant we keep on contract from the CDC, and he told me that everything in real life is measured by work experience. He suggested that I go to night classes and get a degree in law or a master's degree in public health. He thought it would be a waste of time going to a conventional daytime university with all my experience. What do you think?"

"I don't know," Caanen said, shrugging his shoulders.

Evers's cell phone chimed in with a fragment of "Eine kleine Nachtmusik." He flipped it open. "You found it! Thanks, Testfaye. Bring it over and call and arrange for Jeff and Zeleka to come tonight to Fasika."

Evers leaned toward Caanen and continued, "You'll come, right? It's an authentic Ethiopian restaurant with dancing." Evers carefully began brushing the front of his jacket with the back of his hand.

Testfaye greeted Caanen in the parking lot. "Over here, Doktor!" he called.

The two drove back to Hotel Leopol.

THE LEFT HAND

Caanen entered the hotel bar. It had a thick cobalt blue shag carpet. The couches were covered with a fabric sporting zebra-skin designs. He ordered a bottle of Axumit from the young woman behind the bar. He sipped the cold, sweet red wine and began to entertain calling Evers and declining the evening soiree. After a second glass of Axumit, he gave up the idea and resigned himself to spending an evening with Evers.

That evening, Caanen walked to the restaurant, careful to avoid the potholes filled with sheep and donkey dung. The restaurant was a large, traditional Ethiopian hut with tables at the perimeter and several tall poles supporting the high, thatched center of the building. One man played a single-stringed guitar, while several young women outfitted in traditional garb danced in the center of the room. Caanen saw Evers out of the corner of his eye. Evers raised his arm in greeting, and Caanen walked to the table.

"Dr. Caanen, this is Zeleka, and this fellow is Jeff, the newest member of our staff. Zeleka joined us from Brown University, and Jeff is our laboratory procurement officer. The girl who had his job quit last week. This is Julie, a volunteer like you who'll be going to Lalibela. Please, sit down."

"How are you, Dr. Caanen?" asked Julie. She was a registered nurse scheduled to fly to Lalibela and supervise a new clinic. She came from Albuquerque, where she managed an outreach program for HIV patients. She was in her early fifties, half Cheyenne with long black hair. Her eyeglasses were studded with rhinestones and hung by a chain on her full bosom. Caanen felt at ease with her. She was also staying at the Hotel Leopol.

Zeleka was a vivacious, tall Ethiopian American dressed in a discreet, knee-length skirt and high heels. Caanen marveled at how she must have traversed the last one hundred yards of unpaved roadway to the restaurant in those shoes. Jeff was tall and thin with blond hair and a tuft of fuzz on his chin. He was wearing chino trousers and Nike gym shoes. All the Foundation employees lived together in a large, old frame house complete with cooks, housekeepers, and the twenty-four-hour-a-day ministrations of Testfaye.

"Have you eaten *injera* before?" asked Evers, leaning toward Caanen and Julie. He was wearing a blue blazer with large brass buttons and carefully polished black loafers, which he dandled before everyone while crossing his legs. "The *injera* here is excellent. It's made from *tef*, a grain that grows only in Ethiopia. It is said to have a great deal of iron. When the plate arrives, I caution you—there is one grave mistake you can make in Ethiopia, and that is to use your left hand to eat. Here the left hand is reserved for other bodily functions, not eating." He paused for effect. "A word to the wise."

The waitress arrived with a large metal platter with *injera* spread over the surface and auxiliary rolls of *injera* placed at the edge. She poured different meats and sauces onto the *injera* and everyone seated around the table reached with their right hands, tearing off pieces of the bread to pick up bits of meat and sauce.

Jeff informed Caanen that he had left the University of Florida before finishing his first year to join the Dutton Foundation. His job was to ensure that the laboratory equipment was properly supplied and maintained at the clinics.

Caanen asked what experience he'd had with lab equipment.

"None, but I did well in college chemistry, so I think it will be okay. Incidentally," Jeff added, "Mom and Dad are coming to visit me this weekend."

Evers appeared to be the oldest of the Dutton employees. Zeleka and Evers carried on a private conversation between the two of them the remainder of the evening, the theme being that the cleaning ladies at their communal house had mistakenly taken Zeleka to be Evers's girlfriend. Evers took great pains to explain this contretemps.

"It's weird they'd even consider we'd have such an arrangement," said Evers.

"Thank you! I'm sure," said Zeleka sarcastically.

As Caanen looked around at the group, he began to formulate possible Foundation mottos, such as Bright Youth Working Together or We Accept Only the Brightest.

Interrupting Caanen's reveries, Julie said, "Hey, Caanen, I'm left-handed and almost made a major faux pas several times tonight. Evers would be pissed with me."

Evers interrupted the two of them. "Tomorrow night we are celebrating the arrival of some new workers, and one member of our team is going away—he's completed a monthlong internship here, and we're having a dinner for him on Mount Entoto. Would you two like to come?"

Now is not the time to act boorish, particularly in front of all the young guests, Caanen thought. "Yes, I'll go," he said.

"Me, too," said Julie hesitantly.

THE MUSEUM GUIDE

The following morning, Caanen entered the Hotel Leopol dining room. The maître d' stood at the entrance dressed in a dark suit and tie; the cuffs of his jacket were threadbare and shiny from repeated ironing. He leaned over and with pen in hand, struck Caanen's room number off a list, and waved him toward the buffet table. The dining room was large, made to seat several hundred people. Only tables that sat one or two people were in use. The remainder of the tables with their linen tablecloths and napkins were scattered about in this dusty mausoleum.

After coffee, Caanen decided to walk to the City Museum, situated on a hill above Meskel Square, formerly known as Red Square in the country's Communist past. It was a brilliant, sunny morning. Jomo Kenyatta Boulevard was clogged with taxis, minibuses, and larger vehicles spouting diesel fumes that obscured pedestrians' vision. Caanen kept smacking his lips to remove the taste of petrol. The noise from music stores was deafening. Each store had a speaker pointed toward the boulevard with the volume button pegged at maximum. The result was polyphonic cacophony: reggae, traditional Ethiopian music, and rap competing for the ears of the citizens of Addis Ababa.

Strolling up a slight incline, Caanen felt the effects of the more than eight thousand feet of altitude. He walked past small flocks of fat-tailed sheep to reach the museum crowning the top of the hill. Vultures soared lazily in the welkin above. He entered the museum grounds through a small gateway and was immediately confronted by a yellow-ochre wood, gabled house with multipaned window sashes trimmed in white. This was a jarring change of architecture from the countless corrugated metal-roofed, single-story dwellings he had passed walking to the site. The garden sported an exuberant growth of four-foot-high calla lilies and dinner plate-sized zinnias. The grounds were entirely deserted. Caanen walked to the entrance of the building.

He was greeted at the front door by a tall, thin man in his early sixties. He wore a short-billed cap at a jaunty angle on the right side of his head and a shabby, gray wool suit jacket. The elbows and jacket flaps had visible holes. He quickly threw away his cigarette and smiled at Caanen with one tobacco-stained tooth. There was something both elegant and sinister about the man. In the subdued lighting inside the building, it appeared as if this tall specter had stepped out of the nineteenth-century photographs hanging on the museum walls. He immediately began narrating the history of Addis and ushered Caanen from room to room.

"Here is a famous painting of Menelik II. Take a picture! Go ahead, take a picture!" demanded the imperious guide.

For some reason, Caanen did as he was requested, though there was nothing remarkable—either historically or artistically—about the painting of the king on his throne.

The brown tooth reappeared. He lit a cigarette. "Now we go upstairs."

Caanen crept up the wood-plank stairwell where a handful of artifacts were displayed on sagging wooden shelves. They reached the top floor where sun-bleached photos of old roadways and bygone habitations hung on the walls. The paint on the walls was peeling.

The tour came to an end. The guide sidled up to Caanen with one hand in his sagging jacket pocket and the other carelessly waving his cigarette in front of him. He towered over Caanen. Caanen gave him three birr.

The guide suddenly lurched backward in mock disbelief and blurted, "Sir, this is hardly worth it! Surely I did better than this." He held out the three birr and waved them up and down.

Caanen, embarrassed that he had offended the man by offering such a meager tip (eight birr to the dollar), quickly added single bills totaling ten birr into the man's palm. The fellow frowned at him. Caanen reached into his wallet again, removed another ten birr, and pushed them into his palm with emphasis.

"Thank you, sir!" The tobacco-stained tooth reappeared.

Caanen left through the rear of the museum, taking a short cut back to the hotel. He immediately found himself in a stockyard. A few goats and sheep were grazing on meager blades of grass among wooden palings. Ruppell's griffons stood in groups watching two of their fellow birds playing tug-of-war with a strip of sheep offal. They growled, shrieked, and batted their wings at one another. Caanen picked up his pace and sped by the birds, hoping not to be summoned by the museum guide once again. He walked back through Meskel Square toward the soccer stadium.

A huge crowd of men gathered at the stadium railing where one looked down onto a recessed field. Libya was playing Ethiopia. Water covered the field, and the players were splattered with mud. The crowd was wildly cheering every move of the players.

Caanen walked around the perimeter of the crowd and down the boulevard before entering a coffee shop. He was joined almost immediately at the table by a young, dark-skinned man who introduced himself as Mr. Z. Million.

"I imagine you are Christian?" the man asked. He then went into his purpose for sitting down.

"I have a home for what you call 'crazy people.' In Ethiopia, the mentally ill often go naked. I teach them to clothe themselves and obey laws. I need some help—anything you can give me," said Mr.

Million. He spoke excellent English. He was dressed fashionably, but upon closer inspection, it was obvious that the fabrics had never been cleaned. Mr. Million gave Caanen a card with his email address printed on the front.

Caanen paid for their macchiatos and pastry and excused himself to walk back to the hotel.

THE LEPROSARIUM

vers arranged for Testfaye to drive the volunteers to a hospital where the Foundation had established its first HIV clinic. The group consisted of Evers, Caanen, Julie, and a tall, thin physician from Uganda dressed in dark slacks and a black silk shirt adorned with colorful flowers. Testfaye drove up the paved road from the highway to the hospital complex. The roadway was lined with blue gum eucalyptus so densely planted that they usurped the sidewalk, and pedestrians were forced to walk on the road. Testfaye wove the car among the pedestrians, many of them supported by canes and walking sticks fashioned from tree limbs. Numerous buildings were spread over the hilltop. This complex of buildings was formerly the national leprosarium, now converted to an HIV center. It reminded Caanen of Schweitzer's hospital in Lambaréné.

Evers said loudly, "When Dutton came to visit several weeks ago, the Secret Service were worried about this road being so narrow. It could easily be blocked by terrorists. They drove sixty miles per hour up here! Dutton was here for only an hour, and everyone fell in love with him."

They arrived at the clinic, and the volunteers were introduced to the medical director, Dr. Abebe. He had pronounced East African features with a flat nose and round face, rather than the Semitic features characteristic of Ethiopians. He was officially polite, but not friendly, and was dressed in a dark-blue suit, tie, and white shirt. He wore a heavily starched white doctor's jacket with his name embroidered over the left chest pocket. He demonstrated for the guests the typical doctor-patient encounter for HIV patients.

Later, Caanen tried to fathom why this was deemed important. Perhaps the director didn't trust the Ugandan physician to be respectful toward Ethiopian patients. Caanen tried to pay attention, but his eyes wandered to the open window and the volleyball game going on in the quadrangle. Evers was sitting beside Caanen and noticed his lack of attention. He abruptly informed the director that everyone must move on to meet the other clinic members. Caanen courteously shook the director's hand.

The three moved down the hall to meet several more physicians. Two women pediatricians were entering data on laptop computers when the group entered. Evers introduced the group and explained the work the physicians were doing with the children, all of whom had HIV. The young Ugandan doctor, apparently feeling a need to exert himself, began a long recitation of the World Health Organization guidelines regarding HIV drugs for children. He talked without stopping, all the while standing above the two young, petite female physicians.

One of the pediatricians closed her computer cover with a flourish and hastily walked out of the room. The other looked up at the man and grimaced at his manner of delivery. Just what the Foundation was at such great pains to prevent from happening, did occur—the guest physician angering the host country's doctors. The room was silent after the second doctor left the room. Evers was nonplussed.

Caanen noticed a screen saver on one of the computers showing Dutton holding a small child on his lap surrounded by beaming children, nurses, and the two pediatricians who had just left the room.

The visitors then returned to the Hotel Leopol with Testfaye. No one spoke on the return trip.

Later, Julie joined Caanen for a walk along Kenyatta Boulevard. At one street corner, five men were resting at the curb. They had been paralyzed at a young age by polio and were unable to stand. They moved themselves about on their hands, throwing their rigid, useless legs out in front of their torsos.

Julie bit her lower lip. "This is unbelievably depressing."

Children shouted at the two pedestrians. "You! You!" This greeting by Ethiopian children was used for all foreigners, regardless of nationality. Disconcerted by these seemingly rude greetings, Julie nevertheless waved in return. The children smiled and waved back exuberantly.

Julie turned to Caanen and whispered, "These guys walking next to me are scaring me. There's also one on your side. They were standing at the corner when we crossed the street."

Caanen looked to his right where he was accompanied by a tall man with sunken eyes holding a folded newspaper in his hand. Another tall, thin man walked alongside Julie, also holding a newspaper, and stared straight ahead. Caanen grabbed Julie's arm and steered her across the main thoroughfare to a sidewalk that skirted one of the government buildings. Soldiers seated in guard boxes on the hillside next to the building desultorily watched the foot traffic. The two men veered off and ceased to follow them.

Caanen and Julie stood outside a grocery where they purchased bottles of water. Julie was approached by a child of eight with tattered, oily clothing. The cloth at his knees and elbows was worn away. He was barefoot, and there was dirt on his face.

"Birr! Birr! Give me birr!" he said insistently. He grabbed Julie's arm. "Birr! Birr!"

"What should I do?" she asked Caanen

"Don't do anything, or we'll never get rid of him," Caanen said.

"I can't do that. Look at the sores on his arms and legs. He looks starved!" She handed the boy ten birr.

He shrieked, tears lined his cheeks, and he grasped her arm and held onto it throughout the remainder of the walk to the hotel compound.

Julie looked over at Caanen, winced, and gave the child ten more birr. She fled into the hotel foyer with shouts of "You! You!" trailing after her.

Caanen pondered a large advertisement for pest control services at the entrance to the hotel. On the sign were fantastical renditions of a purple cockroach and a rat. Caanen recalled a chapter from the *Lonely Planet* guidebook describing the street boys as the biggest "pests" in Ethiopia.

TOP VIEW RESTAURANT

Testfaye picked up Caanen and Julie at the hotel and drove them to the Dutton Foundation mansion where Evers, Zeleka, and the other employees lived. Like the City Museum, it was a wooden, gabled structure with twenty rooms, surrounded by a screened porch. It was in its stage of dotage and badly needed a coat of paint. The five-acre grounds were unkempt with the exception of a circular garden in the driveway filled with flowering marigolds.

Testfaye led Julie and Caanen to the porch. Evers was busy pacing back and forth while talking into his cell phone. A maid offered them a drink. Caanen took a glass of white wine, a rarity judging from the Hotel Leopol's refreshment list. Evers gave Testfaye some last-minute instructions for the evening and then turned to his two guests and conversed about recruiting good people to join the Dutton Foundation's efforts in Ethiopia. Evers eventually excused himself and left for the restaurant.

Sometime later, Testfaye drove Caanen and Julie up Mount Entoto, where it was dark. The road was winding, and the engine labored. After the car expired in third gear, Testfaye turned the key, restarted the engine, and drove the remainder of the distance in first gear.

"I will give you a call when I want to go back," Caanen directed.

"Yes, Doktor," Testfaye said, looking at Caanen in the rearview mirror.

Caanen and Julie entered the restaurant. To the left was a long trestle table with a dozen people seated along the window side of the table. In the middle of the group was Evers who waved to Caanen. Evers began to introduce the guests. Caanen's seat faced the windows. Except for a few flashing telecommunication poles on the mountainside, there were no lights visible outside of the restaurant. He was disappointed that he could not see Addis at night from the restaurant. Caanen turned his attention to his host. Evers was introducing many of the same office workers whom he had seen the day before at the Domby building.

"And this is Zeleka, whom you met last night," said Evers.

"Yes, I remember."

She was a bit taller than Caanen remembered from the previous night. Her mother was Ethiopian, and her father was a Boston Brahmin. Zeleka was dressed in a short-sleeved blouse with a broad, bare bodice decorated with pewter jewelry. Her exposure of skin other than her arms seemed risqué for Ethiopian women, even in the capitol. She was enrolled in a Master of Public Health program at Brown University and was to be in Addis for several months. Caanen shook her hand across the table.

"Nice to see you again," he said.

The discussion picked up again among the others. Julie and Caanen each drank a cup of tea.

The young man being feted that evening laughed and said, "I got about ten pages written on my thesis last month. So everything wasn't a total bust."

Caanen ate tough tournedos of beef along with fancy mini carrots and squash, both barely heated. The vegetables were exceedingly difficult to cut with a knife.

Talk at the table continued unabated. Caanen could no longer understand the conversation due to the low rumbling sound from the air conditioner and gave himself up to his own reveries. He thought about watercolor sketches he hoped to accomplish while in Ethiopia.

One of the other male guests seated next to Evers leaned over toward him and said, "I've got to get some more leather goods before going back. I'm going to the market in the morning. I'll be in the office sometime in the afternoon."

"Okay," Evers said. He then turned his attention to Caanen. "Well, Doc, when you get to Dessie, we're counting on you boosting the numbers of patients on HIV meds. You do that, and Dutton will be happy."

Caanen could feel a dislike of Evers growing within himself.

Julie remarked under her breath to Caanen, "I can't take any more. These teenagers believe they're running the country. And maybe they are! Let's go to the restroom and get out of here."

Outside the restaurant, Julie turned to Caanen. "What have we signed up for?"

Caanen called Testfaye, and the three drove silently down Mount Entoto.

HIGHLANDS

From Entoto the way led down to a wide plain ...
The route was uneventful, broken only by occasional
clusters of tukals, surrounded by high hedges of
euphorbia. It was very hot ... I fell into a light doze.

—Evelyn Waugh in *Remote People*

The following morning Caanen loaded his traveling bag into the back of the Toyota Land Cruiser, the vehicle of choice of all NGOs in Ethiopia. Testfaye was driving him to Dessie and brought several liters of bottled water for the trip.

The drive began in light rainfall. Testfaye chose a shortcut through Addis passing by the abattoir. The glistening metal roofs of the slaughterhouse were silhouetted against the sky, and every gable was crowded shoulder to shoulder with large, wet, dark vultures. They were keeping a close eye on the comings and goings below them. The drive was uneventful until they reached the outskirts of the city where rural folk clotted the roadway along with their sheep and donkeys.

The vehicle began to descend the mountainside. Suddenly, the sun made its appearance, and Caanen was taken aback by the panoramic vistas on both sides of the road. Luxuriant, green rolling hills rose thousands of feet above the road level. There were scattered huts, and nearby, small children shepherded flocks of sheep and goats. Caanen recognized some of the views as those he had seen in the photographs at the City Museum. In ungrazed areas, flowering *addis abebe*, the national flower, turned the meadows yellow-gold. Children were selling yellow nosegays by the roadside.

Several hours later, Testfaye and Caanen were making their way in light rainfall again. The altitude was more than twelve thousand feet, and the interior of the car was cold. The Addis Ababa to Asmara road was built by Italians during their short occupation in the 1930s. It followed the contours of the land skillfully. Testfaye negotiated a hairpin turn at one point, revealing a breathtaking view of a three-arch bridge rising 80 feet above a rushing stream.

Shortly after crossing the bridge, Testfaye stopped the car in a dense fog. He shifted in the driver's seat and waved toward the back, saying, "Over there's a cliff. Highest in Ethiopia. Be careful. I wait here."

Caanen got out of the car and made his way gingerly through the fog in the direction Testfaye had indicated. The closely cropped grass was oozing moisture. Out of the whitish-gray fog, a young man suddenly approached Caanen with a handful of woolen caps.

"You want?" he asked.

Looking over the man's shoulder, Caanen saw the fog part, revealing a view through a wedge of colossal rocks to a valley thousands of feet below. The precipice fell abruptly from between two walls of stone. On the floor of a valley was a sunlit village surrounded by eucalyptus trees. Hunched up by a boulder at the cliffside was a large rock hyrax, a rodent-like animal, one of the reservoirs of leishmaniasis, a common illness in the Ethiopian Highlands. Caanen shivered and sprinted back to the car.

Testfaye turned the key in the ignition and drove carefully through the fog and rain. At this altitude, they were enveloped in low-lying clouds. Twenty minutes later, the car passed through a quarter-mile-long tunnel and plunged into a different world; now they were in a dry, sunlit valley. *Tukuls* were scattered in tight-knit groups around the mountainsides. Small plots of grain crisscrossed the mountains with swatches of yellow, olive green, and bright green. It rarely rained here. The valley floor was hot. Camels walked along the roadside.

They passed a large, dry riverbed, and Testfaye pulled the car into a clump of towering trees. A motel was nestled in the bush next to the river. This had undoubtedly been a caravansary in years past. The motel rooms were arranged around the restaurant and placed on one long slab of concrete. The doors to the hotel rooms were open. Flies could be seen resting on the white walls, trying to escape the direct sun. The two men walked to the restaurant. A large tree near the restaurant was crowded with marabou storks, some snapping their bills loudly.

Caanen walked to the bathroom. The acrid stench from the latrine brought tears to his eyes. Caanen washed his hands in a trickle of water and hastily walked to his table.

The waiter shooed several parti-colored goats away from the patio and handed menus to the men. After three hours of bouncing and jostling in the car, they had both developed an appetite.

The heat felt soothing after hours of cold rain and fog. Testfaye ordered for both of them—he had been here before. "The pasta is good," he said.

The waiter brought linguine pasta with a dollop of butter on it and tomato paste in silver-plated sauce dishes. The flies unglued themselves from the bedroom walls and moved toward the diners. The goats began creeping back onto the patio and stretched and pulled with their tongues at the tops of rhododendrons growing along the iron railing near Caanen's elbow. The two men began to eat faster.

Testfaye rubbed his palms together and announced, "We go now or never get there, Doctor."

A camel caravan blocked the gateway, and Testfaye could not turn the car onto the roadway. Slowly, haughtily, the animals undulated past. Caanen had to bend down in the front seat in order to see the towering animals with their enormous eyes, long eyelashes, and iconic profiles.

Testfaye stopped one more time on the way to Dessie. Caanen photographed tubular beehives hanging from tall shade trees and weaver bird nests decorating a barren, leafless tree. Caanen watched a young boy walk to a nearby water hole where cattle and goats stood in the water. The boy removed a large water urn from his shoulder and scooped up water and sediment to take back to his thatched hut for drinking water.

At one point, the road paralleled a large marsh with a slow-moving stream. An African fish eagle perched on a large stump by the stream and watched the foot traffic alongside the road.

Just outside the Dessie city limits, the left rear tire blew out. Testfaye skillfully replaced the flat, refusing to allow Caanen to help.

They finally arrived at the Dessie Piazza under a darkening sky. It was a scene straight out of a Turner seascape—a yellow-orange inferno of a horizon with incandescent bulbs shining like circular rainbows through the diesel fumes. Shades of pedestrians darted in front of the headlights. They made their way slowly to Tossa Pension at the northern edge of town. Testfaye brought the room keys from the office and handed one to Caanen, who went up the curving outside stairwell and opened his door. He looked around the eight-by-twelve-foot cubicle that would be his home for months to come. There was an adjoining bathroom with shower and a flush toilet. This was the newest hotel in the city, a two-story structure superficially much like any motel in the States. The doors to the rooms had no weather stripping, and there were no screens on the windows. Mosquitoes terrorized the inhabitants at night, and exotic insects walked on the ceilings. Caanen began taking out his clothing. There was a knock on the door.

"Yes!" Caanen shouted through the wooden door.

"Dr. Caanen? It's Floyd Handel. I work in the clinic."

Caanen opened the door to greet a short, smartly dressed man in a black rain jacket and heavy-soled black shoes. He sported a carefully trimmed moustache and beard. His short, graying hair was worn in a crew cut. His cheeks were hollow.

"Um, I'm glad you're here," said Floyd. " I'll knock on your door tomorrow, and we can walk to breakfast. Is that okay with you?"

Caanen knew that Floyd was working at the clinic and had already been in Dessie three months. He followed Floyd to his room.

"I have been getting sort of homesick lately," Floyd said.

"Well, I can understand that," said Caanen.

Floyd's closet of a room was piled high with suitcases and brown paper bags stuffed with gifts for friends back home. Floyd lit a cigarette, and the two shared their cell phone numbers. Caanen said good night and retired to his room.

It rained lightly all night. The nightclub next door to the hotel issued forth a constant drumbeat that reverberated within the motel room. Just when Caanen was drifting off to sleep, he was awakened by the nearby call of hyenas. They patrolled the streets nightly. He was awakened one more time in the early-morning hours, this time by the call of a nearby muezzin.

THE CLINIC

F loyd came to Caanen's room at seven in the morning. The two men walked through the gate leading to the pension and onto the street. Behind the pension was an enormous flat-topped mountain, Mount Tossa. It was shrouded by clouds and looked foreboding. It was cold, and light rain was falling. Fog hung about in the low spots. Toyota minibuses patrolled the main roadway next to the pension.

Floyd wanted to walk to Aytegeb Café, a mile from the pension. "Is that okay with you?" he asked.

"Sure. I need the exercise after yesterday's endless drive from Addis," Caanen said.

Caanen pulled the hood of his jacket over his head. The two walked for twenty minutes in light rain to Aytegeb Café and ordered breakfast. Aytegeb was the newest restaurant in the city. It had large windows in front and a patio facing the main north-south road. Dessie boasted a population of 160,000 people according to the 2005 census. The restaurant was on the main roadway and was frequented almost daily by whites who worked for the numerous NGOs headquartered in the city.

Floyd complained that he ordered French toast every morning at the restaurant, and regardless of his order, he was always served a scrambled egg sandwich with ketchup, lettuce, and French fries.

Caanen ordered eggs with meat, and Floyd ordered French toast, directing the waitress's attention to the picture of French toast on the menu.

The waitress served scrambled egg sandwiches to both of them five minutes later.

Floyd laughed derisively as he dashed ketchup onto a slice of bread. "God, I am getting so sick of scrambled egg sandwiches."

Caanen glanced out the window at what was now a surging rainfall. Rain was falling obliquely against the windowpanes. The television in the restaurant showed film footage of flooded areas in northern Ethiopia. More than two hundred people had drowned in the country because of floods in the past month.

Floyd finished his egg sandwich and said, "Let's get going."

There was little activity on the road as they walked to the hospital. Floyd stopped at a roadside shop and purchased a package of Rothmans. He lit his cigarette, and the smoke trailed out the side of his rain hood. They trudged on in the rain, their pant legs wet to the knees and the soles of their footgear caked with mud and dung. Caanen's Gortex jacket even began to leak, and rivulets of water ran down the back of his neck. Two-wheeled jitneys pulled by undernourished horses known as *garis* plied the roadway. Water running off banana leaves and rusting rooftops plashed onto the pavement.

Suddenly, out of nowhere, a stark-naked young woman with a wild, terrified look in her eye raced past the two men going in the same direction in the middle of the road.

"You'll see her every now and then," Floyd said, unfazed.

They arrived at the entrance to the hospital grounds and walked beneath the metal arch with the name Dessie Referral Hospital painted in red, both in Amharic and English. They walked down a steep drive to the hospital building. It had been constructed during the final days of Haile Selassie's reign. Made of granite blocks decoratively chiseled en face, it was the first such building Caanen had seen since leaving Addis. Like so much of Ethiopia, the hospital seemed frozen in time.

The electricity was not working that morning, and the cleaning women had not started work for the day. There was blood on the floor of the foyer. They walked through the hospital corridors, which were packed elbow to elbow with family members of patients. Some of the visitors had AK-47s strapped to their shoulders.

Floyd and Caanen gently pushed their way through the family groups that thronged the main hallway. A physician in a white jacket caught Caanen's attention. He was walking ahead of them in a loping gait. His right leg was permanently bent at the knee at a forty-five-degree angle, requiring him to flow up and down while walking, the foot barely striking the ground.

Caanen and Floyd exited through a wooden door fastened by leather hinges and walked out into the rain. Twenty yards farther, they arrived at the clinic. There was corrugated tin roofing over a twenty-by-twenty-foot space of uneven ground punctuated with large boulders. Patients lay on the damp ground under blankets. Others stood patiently in the rain. Hospital guards dressed in khaki and wearing saucer caps stood on either side of the entrance to the clinic building.

Floyd remarked, "This is the clinic, and these are the patients. There are around a hundred a day. They issue medical records at the desk, and then the patient stands in line to see the doctor."

The two walked into the clinic building.

"This is Dr. Abdul, one of the doctors in the clinic. He has been working here for about a week."

Abdul was tall, thin, and well-dressed; he had a moustache and beard shaved pencil-thin, the beard coming across his jaw above the edge of his chin, a style among some Muslims. Abdul's smile showed straight, white teeth.

"No one likes this assignment, especially the young doctors, like Abdul. They're assigned for one year to the hospital by the government," said Floyd.

"How are you, Dr. Robert?" Abdul said. "Maybe we can talk about this patient. I am not sure about the skin rash."

Caanen took off his jacket, hung it on the coat rack, and sat down in a chair alongside Abdul's desk. They spent the morning and afternoon going over patient histories and discussing diagnosis and therapy. Abdul had little experience with HIV. Caanen's job was to mentor the doctors in the art and science of HIV patient care.

"It is pretty hopeless, don't you think, Dr. Robert?" Abdul asked. "I mean, we can't diagnose much, and we don't have any drugs that we need."

"Well, we'll do what we can. You're starting a lot of patients on therapy, and that's good," said Caanen.

Floyd opened the door to the examination room and entered with his arms full of folded curtains and interrupted their discussion, "Let's get these up, so we won't have to fuss with them tomorrow," he said. The curtains broke up the large room and provided some privacy for the patients.

The clinic guards burst into the room carrying a young woman in her twenties complaining of weakness in her legs and inability to walk. Caanen performed a rapid physical examination. Her reflexes were very brisk in her lower extremities, but she had no sensation below her navel. Caanen discussed the case with Abdul. The two concluded that she had inflammation of the spinal cord due to HIV. She was later sent home with her relatives and antiretroviral medications.

Caanen looked out the window at the fifty or so patients squatting on the ground beneath the corrugated roof. A young woman was lying by herself on the moist ground. Caanen approached the woman and leaned over her. The guard who accompanied him said that she was pregnant and bleeding. The two carried her into the office. A strong, fetid odor permeated the room. Caanen lifted her dress as she shifted her buttocks so that he could see the problem. There were enormous, cauliflower-sized genital warts on her vulvar region. Blood was seeping around the edges of the growths.

The patient lay on the examination table and wept silently. She accidentally dropped a plastic bag containing all of her possessions. There were several birr notes, coins, and an assortment of pills scattered on the concrete floor. She had traveled from Addis Ababa by foot after being told there was nothing that could be done for her. Caanen admitted her to the gynecology ward for the night. The patients waiting at the clinic were told to come back in the afternoon.

Another seventy-five patients were seen that afternoon. The women sat quietly on the ground. Some of the men formed a line at the door, jostling with one another for a better position as they waited to see the doctor.

Floyd was busy from the time of arrival to the closing of the clinic doors. Nurses, pharmacists, and many young doctors quizzed him on what should be done in the clinic, everything from drapes and drug refills for the HIV patients to where to dispose of used needles and dirty linen. He was obviously indispensible.

After mentoring Dr. Abdul all afternoon, Caanen walked back to the pension. Across the street from the pension, trailers lined the roadway, each with an open side flap where their wares were displayed. Caanen bought several oranges, chocolate bars, and bottled water. He walked into the office of the pension to retrieve his key. There was only one key to each room, and the housekeepers needed it each morning in order to clean and tidy the rooms. The office was in a sizable mansion that had several large suites reserved for various dignitaries associated with NGOs. The hotel rooms were to the rear of this building, comprising two stories of cubicles behind flimsy wooden doors.

FOREWARNING

T he next morning, Caanen and Floyd walked to Aytegeb
Café. Floyd ordered French toast; Caanen ordered *buna*—an
espresso.

Moments later, Caanen glanced up to see Floyd slamming his fist on the table. "Goddamn it! I've had it with these scrambled egg sandwiches," he hollered.

"Floyd, sit down and forget it. We'll eat somewhere else tomorrow."

The waitress looked at Floyd quizzically. His anger subsided.

Both men left the restaurant and walked downhill to the hospital. Men going in the opposite direction were cleaning their teeth with a stick from the toothbrush tree, *Salvatoria persica*. The stick was carved to resemble the end of a screwdriver and was rubbed up and down on the surface of the teeth. It was an effective dentifrice; most Ethiopians had large, beautiful white teeth.

Caanen and Floyd walked to the director's office where Dr. Isaac was giving an in-service lecture. The office walls were painted a watery yellow. Outdated work schedules were taped askew on the walls. Dusty curtains hung over the windows. Abdul and three young physicians were seated on a broken-down divan along with Dr. Mulugeta, the physician with the limp who ran the medical inpatient service. The topic of the lecture was cholera.

"I'm making trips across Ethiopia to let every one know that we've had several recent cases of cholera—one in Addis and another near the Somali border," began Isaac. "We know both cases originated somewhere in the Sudan."

The younger doctors grinned, and Abdul asked, "So what else is new?"

Disregarding Abdul's sarcasm, Isaac continued. "There has been no secondary spread. However, as you know, our government has not always responded in the best way to these challenges in the past. We are trying to do it right this time and notify all the health personnel we can."

Dr. Mulugeta leaned forward in his seat, smiled, and said in knowing fashion, "The problem is if we find anything, will it be reported? I was present for the last outbreak of cholera in '85. That could be repeated again."

Mulugeta was in his late forties with short, grizzled hair, light-brown skin, and a three-day growth of beard. He had on a tie and pressed, white dress shirt. He was originally from Tigray and had moved to Dessie more than twenty years ago. The Tigray people figured prominently in the history of the popular Ethiopian Christian Church. They were a pastoral people, still wedded to using oxen in the field.

"Well, I am trying to get out the word," said Isaac.

"We have cases meeting your definition of cholera every week, and we admit them to the hospital. No one has been interested in looking into this problem before," Mulugeta said.

Dr. Isaac was visibly frustrated and cut his presentation short. He was a vigorous man in his early forties with an easy and gracious manner. He was accustomed to telling others what to do. He repeated that there was no evidence of a cholera epidemic in the country. He remarked that he had traveled to many regions to determine if there were undue numbers of adults being admitted with diarrhea and had found none.

Caanen thought of Aschenbach in *Death in Venice*. He began to wonder whether he might fall prey to some ghastly disease that the locals knew about but was denied by the authorities.

Caanen and Mulugeta walked back to the medical ward together.

"We had three cases of recurrent fever admitted last night. The patients are out here in the hall. They're all street boys," said Mulugeta while undulating alongside Caanen.

Caanen glanced at several ten-year-old boys lying on palettes in the hallway. "Do they have lice?" he asked.

"Everyone here has lice," answered Mulugeta. "You will only see this disease in Ethiopia, Sudan, and Eritrea. We see cases frequently when the weather turns cold."

The two made rounds on the inpatients.

Toward noon, Caanen suddenly felt a gripping sensation in his lower abdomen. The latrine was adjacent to huts used by long-term patients and their families. The small enclosure had a concrete floor with two holes spaced two feet apart, each with a set of raised footprints forward of the hole for the individual to stand upon and squat. There was a slight depression in the floor and urine stagnated several inches deep. Caanen fought off the flies, relieved himself, and vowed never to use the latrine again. He walked to the pension and stayed close to the toilet for the remainder of the afternoon.

HOSPITAL ROUNDS

The following day, Caanen and Floyd walked to the Ghion Hotel for breakfast. This was a mile-long walk similar to that of Aytegeb, but farther up the face of Mount Tossa. The hotel was built by two Italian women during Italy's occupation of Abyssinia. Some of the original china dinnerware was still in use. The two men sat in the dining room where sunlight coursed through the tall windows and yellowing sheer curtains billowed outward with each slight breeze. Floyd ordered scrambled eggs. Caanen ordered toast and coffee. Ali waited on them. He was dressed in frayed formal black attire, and his white shirt was soiled at the cuffs.

"God, this is a good egg. I'll have a *buna* too," said Floyd, lighting up a cigarette.

"This is a nice relief from the noise at Aytegeb," said Caanen.

"I have to take Benjamin and Zirro to school first thing this morning," Floyd said. "I'm meeting with their teachers." Floyd had 'adopted' Benjamin and Zirro and was paying for their schooling. Each boy was about sixteen years of age.

Caanen questioned the wisdom of Floyd adopting and escorting teenage boys around town, even though it was customary for young Ethiopian men to walk about holding hands. Caanen started for the hospital, and Benjamin and Zirro joined Floyd outside the hotel and walked farther up Mount Tossa to the school.

Caanen went on rounds with Mulugeta. There were thirty-five inpatient beds, and the majority of the patients had HIV. Mulugeta's grizzled beard belied his underlying good humor.

"You remember her, don't you? Pregnant. Anemic. Her hematocrit is 6 percent. We'll give her two units of blood," Mulugeta said, approaching the bed.

Caanen recognized the young woman that he had admitted several days ago with large warts on the genitalia.

"Is there any malaria?" asked Caanen

"No." Mulugeta moved on to the next bed.

"This patient has HIV. She is on antiretrovirals and has a pleural effusion, probably TB." Mulugeta turned toward the chief nurse who stood by him. "Sister, give me an eighteen-gauge needle and a syringe."

He took the syringe from the nurse and fastened the needle to the hub. He wiped the rib cage with a cotton swab soaked in iodine solution and asked the patient to hold her breath. He inserted the needle to the hub beneath her armpit and slowly withdrew the syringe while aspirating a clear straw-yellow fluid. The patient did not flinch or cry out.

"No pus," Mulugeta said, removing the syringe. "Sister, start her on TB therapy."

The chief nurse wrote the orders on a slip of paper and handed it to the patient's husband so he could take the prescription to the hospital pharmacy and purchase the drugs.

The chief nurse pushed the cart containing all the patient records into an adjoining room.

"This patient has cryptococcal meningitis and a bad headache. Let's do a lumbar puncture." Mulugeta then prepped the lower back with iodine solution and inserted an eighteen-gauge needle directly into the lumbar region. Clear fluid began to drip from the needle hub. "I'll take lots of fluid off, and she'll feel better."

The hospital beds were little more than a frame with a one-inch-thick mattress covered with a rubberized sleeve. Patients brought their own blankets. The gray walls were pitted, and the curtains partially covering the windows were dirty and water-stained following years of use. The stench from the unwashed patients and their clothing caused the uninitiated to retch. Caanen's stomach felt queasy.

Caanen left for the clinic, meeting Dr. Wondersson in the corridor. Wondersson was a good friend of Abdul and worked in the clinic as well as the emergency room.

"How are you doing, Wondersson?" Caanen asked. "I haven't seen you for several days."

"Oh my goodness, Dr. Robert, I've been busy in the emergency room. Today, they brought in a lot of car accident victims. I just finished with them. Oh my God—what a lot of work that was."

"Do you need some help?" said Caanen.

"No."

END OF THE DAY

W

alking home from the clinic at the end of day was becoming easier, even at nine thousand feet elevation. Leaving the arch at the entrance to the hospital, there was a steep ascent up an asphalt strip to the main north-south thoroughfare. It was cluttered with beggars of all descriptions: older men holding out their hands, bedraggled women with pieces of cloth stretched over their laps, and recently discharged hospital patients with swollen or amputated limbs thrust toward the pedestrians. Caanen huffed up the incline, trying to ignore the beggary. Children called out "You! You!" to get his attention. Sometimes a passerby would clasp his hand in a fond handshake.

Once on the main thoroughfare, he threaded his way past the sleeping dogs clustered around the mechanics working at the bus stop. The dogs, engulfed in clouds of diesel smoke all day long, lay curled up at the edge of the road, their ribs showing and their white spots dotted with oily smut. The mechanics were busy prying tires off hubs and dragging on cigarettes.

The area was used as a car wash. Small boys scooped water from the concrete gutters at the edge of the road and splashed the muddy water against the sides of the vehicles and wiped them down with a rag. Caanen dodged the puddles and dung and continued walking to the pension.

Caanen met Wondersson at the restaurant that evening. He was accompanied by Dr. Abdul. Caanen ordered rice with lamb. The others ordered meat in an injera casing. The latter was served in a covered dish and gently poured on a tray lined with injera. The parcel moved about as if it were alive, the meat shifting in the injera casing.

The discussion turned to politics.

"Our problem is the government here is so corrupt," said Wondersson.

"Your country's not helping by sending all of these NGOs. They're keeping this government in power," said Abdul.

"The only source of money is the NGOs!" said Wondersson, shaking his head. He removed his glasses and cleaned them on his shirtsleeve.

"On top of that, our intellectuals are corrupt. All the university teachers want to do is push around the students, and the professors are doing no research."

Caanen could not deny the impact of the omnipresent NGOs, what with their flashy vehicles and ostentatious office buildings and their sole concern being their own special issues, to the exclusion of all else. This was arrogance.

Caanen walked back to the pension in the dark. Shop owners were closing and locking doors and windows. Caanen carefully dodged the oncoming headlights. The thought of hyenas beginning to roam the alleys made him pick up his pace.

MENDICANTS

T he crowd of patients at the clinic broke up at noon. Floyd and Caanen boarded a minibus for town to go to lunch. The bus stopped at the bottom of a steep hill. They clambered out, paid the child conductor, and started up the hill toward the restaurant. They were immediately confronted by a group of beggars. Several women with missing fingers held out their palms to Caanen.

He gave each woman a coin. This precipitated a storm of protest from the other seated beggars. One man rushed at Caanen with his hand outstretched shouting, "Money! Money!" Caanen threw up his hands in mock exasperation and began to sprint up the hill, waving his arms. The women cackled with laughter, and the other beggars grinned.

My God, Caanen thought, *beggars possess a sense of humor.*

A lone beggar pursued Caanen at a fast pace, his arm outstretched, palm upward. Caanen turned, saw the man trailing behind him, stopped, and gave him a coin. The remaining seated beggars yelled in approval.

Floyd and Caanen walked to the entrance of Kalkadan Restaurant. The doorman jumped from his chair and came to attention. He was wearing a forest-green uniform with gold piping and a saucer cap. He opened the door and waved the customers inside. The entrance was a bright yellow created by *addis abebe* sprinkled about on the threshold. The floor inside the restaurant was strewn with a thick carpet of grass sheaves. They were seated by the waiter who was dressed in an ersatz US Air Force uniform.

The restaurant was two stories high. The restrooms were a flight of stairs lower and located outside. Caanen waited in light drizzle to enter the toilet. He returned to the table and ordered some sautéed greens with a sprinkling of lamb. Floyd ordered the same.

Floyd returned to the hospital immediately after lunch to meet a contingent of office employees from several NGOs. Caanen walked slowly back to clinic. He arrived to find Floyd in the center of a group all talking at once and occupying the patient examination rooms.

ONE MORE NGO

One very tall, thin white man was conspicuous by reason of his bold canary-yellow eyeglass frames. His gray hair was cropped short in a flat top. The powwow involving the visitors was attended by all the young doctors, nurses, and clinic personnel and lasted for two hours. The employees were eager to see if there were better-paying positions with the new NGOs.

The patients, who never failed to gather at the clinic, were forced to stand in a single-file line outside the clinic, holding their record folders. They were all anxious to see the doctor, but most of the rooms were occupied by the crowd of visitors. Caanen frowned and gestured for the patients to follow him to the pharmacy. The visiting nabobs eventually worked their way around to Caanen.

"Hi, I'm Jack Fisk with the AIDS Training Center. I'm here to make sure the records are kept properly,"

Caanen stared fixedly at the opalescent yellow rims of his eyeglasses.

Fisk offered further explanation. "I'm working with the University of California to make sure patients are enrolled and data is entered accurately. We've found out that we're way behind schedule here. I would like the personnel to start working Saturdays and Sundays to catch up."

Floyd joined the two men. "We're the third-largest clinic in the country, but we have only one doctor on duty at any one time. We are working at capacity now. We need more help, not more work," he said.

"Nevertheless, let's try it out. The Center will pay for the overtime," said Fisk.

The clinic personnel liked the idea, because it would provide more income. Floyd and Caanen shook their heads in disbelief.

"They'll burn out," said Floyd.

Caanen saw Dutton Foundation personnel standing behind Fisk. There was Jeff, the laboratory equipment procurer; a young nurse; and Zeleka. Suzie, the nurse, introduced herself to Caanen, offering her right wrist to be shaken, a sign of respect among the Ethiopians. This affectation irritated Caanen coming so unexpectedly from such a young Western woman.

She gushed, "I'm learning so much about HIV. Maybe when I get back, I'll focus on HIV prevention."

Caanen responded with, "Sure. Good idea."

Suzie asked if the clinic functioned well. Caanen was blunt. "The blood chemistry machine has been down for two weeks now. We can't be certain whether we are causing liver damage or not with our medications if we don't have this machine. The machine is the Foundation's responsibility, and no one can seem to get it fixed."

"Doctor, that's why we're here. That's why Jeff has come out into the field," said Suzie. She took down Caanen's comments on a legal pad.

"Well, I don't want to be rude, but we have been waiting for this machine to be fixed. There has to be better planning, not just sending out eager young workers."

"Well, here comes Zeleka, who is innocent of any wrongdoing." Suzie turned to introduce the young woman to Caanen.

"We already know one another," Caanen said as he extended his hand. Zeleka shook it firmly.

After locking the clinic doors at the end of the day, Caanen and Floyd walked slowly into town to meet the visitors once again for dinner at Aytegeb. Floyd handed out several coins to beggars stationed along the roadway.

Fisk hosted the dinner and greeted everyone as they entered the restaurant. Orders were taken. Fisk introduced his wife, who had traveled to Dessie with him. She was on sabbatical leave from teaching elementary school in Northern California. Fisk droned on about his commitment to doing something about HIV and the opportunity he now had to help. He had recently retired from selling electronics. By now, Caanen was used to the unusual explanations for one's presence in Ethiopia and paid scant attention to the table conversation. Floyd, more diplomatic, engaged in small talk.

Wondersson sat next to Zeleka, trying desperately to impress her with emergency room stories. "Oh my God, what a mess that knife fight victim was …"

Zeleka smiled and turned toward Caanen. "We're going to be here several weeks."

Dinner was served. Afterward, Fisk insisted that everyone pay their share of the bill. "I need to keep to my *per diem*," he said.

Caanen grinned and said that he would handle the entire bill. The total came to 67 birr (about eight dollars). All the dinner guests then left for their respective hotels.

FLOYD'S BOYS

Floyd diligently worked on bringing order to the patient record system. There were more than five thousand records. More than one hundred were pulled every morning for clinic. The records were kept on construction paper folded crosswise, and the soft paper was deteriorating from moisture and constant use. Many records were lost. Floyd worked eight hours a day for weeks on end to restore an accurate records system. In between times, he organized a method for the pharmacy to renew medications, something that up to then required writing prescriptions every month for patients who would be taking the medications for years.

Floyd looked around for Desarie, the young man responsible for preparing and filing the patient records. In spite of being paid wages equal to the nurses, he often came in late, hung over, and unapologetic. As the records specialist, he had been hired by another NGO, and his supervisor was only sporadically present. Floyd took Desarie under his wing, convinced he was salvageable. Desarie's behavior reminded Floyd of his own younger days.

One of Desarie's vices was chewing chat, a leaf from a shrub with amphetamine-like properties. There were numerous chat suppliers along the trunk road in Dessie, and the truck drivers were fond of stopping at these makeshift tents where the plant was sold. The tongues of users were stained olive-green.

Desarie was not to be found in the clinic. "Let's wake Desarie up," Floyd said to Caanen.

They walked out of the compound, wending their way through tight alleys. Floyd pushed open a gate made of thin eucalyptus branches. He banged his fist against a heavy wooden door leading into a low shed.

"Just a minute," came from within.

Desarie opened the door a crack. It was so dark one could not make out his features. Floyd pushed the door wide open. Desarie retreated to his bed and got under the covers. A hen squawked and fled outside from under the bed.

"Come on. Get up, Desarie. We'll see you in clinic," said Floyd.

Floyd and Caanen returned to the hospital. Joseph, a ten-year-old orphan living at the hospital, came up to them.

"Floyd is going to send me to a good school so that I can learn English," Joseph informed Caanen with a smile that showed his beautiful white teeth.

"Great, Joseph," said Caanen.

"Can you help with me too, Dr. Robert?"

"We'll see," said Caanen.

Caanen felt guilty because Joseph asked him to help. Joseph had insulin-dependent diabetes and no parents and had suffered more in ten years than Caanen had in a lifetime. Joseph was one of the many family members Floyd had adopted and supported with money. Floyd already had two sons, Zirro and Benjamin, Muslim orphans who accompanied Floyd to dinner every evening and were inseparable from him during the weekends. Although they were sixteen, they already sported well-trimmed moustaches.

"Even when I return home, I plan on sending the boys a hundred dollars a month. What I can't do is provide money for all the others who bang on my door every night," said Floyd.

MONKEY PAWS

L ate that afternoon, Caanen walked downtown. Five roads came together at the piazza located on the highest point in the city. Lighting for the area came from shop windows along the road. A cloud of dust rose from the street and blended into the yellowish sky. He walked into the Internet shop, signed into his email account, and slowly, painstakingly began reading his correspondence. Computers at the shop were served by telephone dial-up. On the odd day, one got lucky, and things moved fairly quickly. On the average day, it took twenty-five minutes or more to respond to one email.

Two elderly women quietly shuffled into the store. They began speaking softly at Caanen's left shoulder. Their shawls were pulled tightly around their heads and shoulders. Their feet were bare. One held out a hand imploringly, showing a henna-stained palm decorated with five small stumps of fingers lost to leprosy. Caanen placed a coin in her palm, and the woman thanked him with a toothless smile.

Caanen swiveled in his chair and went back to reading email. The first two emails were from Z. Million in Addis Ababa who was clothing the insane. "Please, Mr. Caanen. God is working through you to help my patients."

Moments later, he felt a faint touch on his left forearm and glanced over and saw that Monkey Paws had slipped into the shop and stood grinning at Caanen. Monkey Paws was six years of age and lived on the streets. He dressed in flip-flops, dirty dark-green shorts, and a faded red T-shirt. Every visitor to Dessie came to know Paws at some point. He was ubiquitous in the downtown area.

"Hi, Paws. Watch out for the store guy." Caanen cocked his head toward the young man behind the counter.

Monkey Paws grinned and shook his head. He held out his right hand. "Birr, birr," he cooed.

The young man at the counter recognized Paws and started for him. Paws put up his thin arms and danced out the front door like a dervish, taunting the clerk. Caanen settled back to his email. Suddenly, there was a shriek from one of the girls behind the counter. Caanen looked up to see Monkey Paws peeing on the front door of the Internet shop. Urine was flowing down the glass pane. Paws grinned and scampered off.

That evening as Caanen walked back to his pension with Monkey Paws beside him, a man dressed in a suit and tie suddenly came out of a dark alley and kicked at Monkey Paws. Caanen waved the fellow off. The man scowled, charged toward Caanen, and gestured with his arms and said in perfect English, "This is my country, and I know the problems these boys cause. Please, sir! Let me handle this!"

Caanen offered a conciliatory gesture as Monkey Paws scampered away.

GUTEN MORGEN

A fter his arrival in Dessie, morning ablutions were a trial for Caanen. He recalled the admonition of his Chief of Infectious Diseases back in the States who warned Caanen that he should wear shoes everywhere in Africa. The number of parasitic infections one could contract through exposure to the soil was astronomical. The hotel provided a pair of petite flip-flops that barely covered the ball of his foot. Caanen was assiduous in wearing the flip-flops at all times in his room, limping about and pinching the slippers between his toes to keep them on his feet. When he returned at night, he was careful to remove his boots close to the door and thus not scatter the dirt about. He imagined parasite eggs breaking loose from the soil and the young worms penetrating his feet.

Caanen left for Aytegeb Restaurant for breakfast alone. There were several Ethiopians in the restaurant sipping *buna*. After the waitress delivered his coffee, Caanen gazed out the window toward the main street. Several men were digging holes alongside the road, preparing to install a fence in front of the restaurant and the adjoining businesses.

"Morgen!"

Caanen looked up at a tall, blond man standing before him.

"Hello," said Caanen.

"Are you from the States? My name is Gunther. I'm an engineer."

"Yes, I am from the States. I'm working at the hospital. Do you live in Dessie?" Caanen asked.

"Ja, we're gone much of the time to Somalia, but we live in the apartment house you pass every day near the Hotel Ghion."

Caanen knew the building the man was referring to. It was the newest structure on the street. He recalled seeing Gunther sitting in front of a computer in a glassed-in office on the ground floor.

"What sort of work are you doing?" asked Caanen.

"We advise people on how to make government buildings all over Africa. Enjoy the coffee. It's excellent. We'll see you around," Gunther said.

Caanen returned to watching the work on the retaining fence and sipping his *buna*. Several barefoot municipal workers carried prewelded pieces of fencing and plunged the poles into the holes they had dug. The fence was apparently intended to provide protection for those walking alongside the road from errant cars. Little thought had gone into the material to build the fence. The fence line was askew. It would only further discommode the pedestrians.

INFECTION CONTROL

Caanen walked under the entrance arch toward the hospital and saluted the guards. The main pathway to the hospital was covered with black, shining granite cobblestone, each stone eight to ten inches wide with course edges. It was slippery and rugged walking, especially when wet. The administrative building was a flat-roofed affair by the side of the path. Grass was lush and waist high. There were dirt trails going to the various outbuildings, the most well trodden leading to the coffee shop.

The hospital was one story high. The back of the hospital accommodated a tuberculosis ward. A new wing was being constructed on the west side of the hospital where a crew of twenty men and women worked daily on the project. Concrete slabs were poured for the walls of the new edition. Part of the crew was breaking apart granite boulders with sledges, and the fragments were picked up by a crew of women, carried to the building, and tamped level with the soil in preparation for laying concrete over the rock stratum.

Caanen walked around to the back of the hospital and passed the incinerator, which stood as a silent reminder of bygone standards. It was a well-made brick structure with a fifty-foot chimney and a strong cast-iron door. Off to the side of the incinerator was a smoldering fire where all the hospital refuse was carried each day and dumped. The pile of trash had been accumulating since the incinerator ignition wiring malfunctioned five years earlier. Several thick-billed ravens picked through the trash. A small boy retrieved a rubber ball from the pile. Intravenous needles and plastic tubing lay scattered about with blood-soaked gauze pads.

Later, Caanen walked through the surgery waiting area. Two nurses were pushing a gurney with a bare metal surface smeared with blood. They helped a patient from a bench onto the gurney who lay back on the surface covered with another's blood.

Caanen proceeded on to the clinic to sit with Abdul and go over patients' histories. One hundred people were scattered around the building waiting to be seen. They refused to stand in line and rushed toward the entrance at every opportunity. When Caanen left to retrieve a record, he had to forcibly push aside the waiting patients.

At about ten o'clock, Caanen walked over to the hospital to make rounds with Mulugeta and was joined by Zeleka. She was a little overdressed for the occasion with a red dress, wide black belt, and shiny loafers. She had no visible jewelry this time.

"Hi, Dr. Caanen. How are you?"

"Going to make rounds with us?" he asked.

"I thought I would see what it's like," she said. "I'm thinking maybe I should become a doctor. Maybe when I return to Boston, I'll apply for medical school."

"Fine, Zeleka," said Caanen, dodging two women pushing a cumbersome and creaking cart down the hallway as they doled out gruel to patients. Patient meals never varied; a mash or soup was served three times a day. The steam rising from the large vat gave off an odor of spiced lentils. Ramadan was fast approaching, and Caanen wondered about the lack of food that would ensue during the day for many patients.

They went to the medicine office where they were met by Mulugeta. Several patients lay on examination tables, too weak to raise their heads.

"Find a bed for them in the ward, Sister," Mulugeta said. He looked quizzically at Zeleka.

Caanen introduced Zeleka to Dr. Mulugeta, and the three of them set out to make rounds on thirty inpatients.

The heat was oppressive that morning. The patient odor in the rooms clung to the bedding and the walls. One of the last patients they rounded upon was the young pregnant woman from Addis Ababa with the cauliflower warts around her genitalia. She was a little stronger, and there was less bleeding. The gruel was providing her nutrition. She pulled up her nightgown to show the doctors the lesions. Her abdomen was more swollen than before.

Zeleka grimaced and leaned backward. Mulugeta frowned at her.

Caanen walked to the sink, turned on the weak stream of water, and washed his hands with the remnants of a bar of soap.

"Why don't you and I go for a coffee, Zeleka?"

The two walked to the coffee shop near the compound entrance.

"Well, I feel guilty for feeling so queasy, but the smell is awful," Zeleka said.

"It's okay. I had the same feelings when I began here. The trick is to stay with it. You don't smell anything after a while," Caanen explained.

"Maybe I could come back and help some day?" Zeleka stated.

"Sure, any time," Caanen said as he swallowed the remainder of his *buna.*

At noon, Zeleka and Caanen took a minibus downtown. They stepped out and walked up the hill to Hotel Ghion. Ali came from behind the bar to seat them in the dining room. They talked discursively about the patients and the lack of resources at the hospital. Several Ethiopians were seated in the lounge smoking and sipping *buna.*

DR. ISAAC

Saturday morning, Dr. Isaac called Caanen on his cell phone. Would he like to come over to his house and have dinner with his wife and son? Caanen said that he would. Zeleka was to join them at his house.

Isaac walked to Caanen's pension and then accompanied him on foot the two miles back to his house. It had rained the evening before, and the sides of the road were muddy and slippery. Caanen was dressed in jeans and a jacket. Isaac had on fine dress slacks, a clean white shirt, and black leather shoes.

Isaac talked about his work with the World Health Organization.

"I have been with them for five years. That's enough. I'm trying to find a place to practice pediatrics on my own. I'm going to Kombolcha this week to look for an office."

"Do you like your work with WHO?" Caanen asked.

"Well, I used to. Not anymore. I am away from home five weeks out of every six. It's getting old."

"What do you do on the trips?" asked Caanen.

"Generally, the office in Addis gets notification of cases of diarrhea from a regional hospital. I go to the hospital and go through the records, looking for possible cases of polio or cholera. Those are the two diarrheal diseases that WHO is interested in. I find out where the patient lives, and then I make my way to the village. This sometimes takes days of hiking. There are usually no roads, so I can't drive there. I sleep in the thatched huts with the people's lice and eat their food. Even though I carry a lot of water in the car, sometimes I'm forced to drink village water. I frequently get diarrhea myself. When I find a patient, I take a fecal sample and try and isolate the bacterium. This goes on month after month."

He continued, "What galls me is that there are many WHO conferences being held all the time in Europe and elsewhere. I have never once been asked to attend one conference, yet all of the front office staff in Addis go to Europe several times a year to conferences. But not me!"

The two colleagues made their way on a muddy path to a compound with a well-constructed single-level home. Isaac's wife greeted them at the door. She was attractive with short, bobbed hair and wore a traditional, colorful garment, around which a young boy entwined his arms. In a short time, Zeleka joined them, arriving by taxi.

Isaac served beer and handmade rice snacks. His wife set up a small table in the living room and spread *addis abebe* and sheaves of grass on the floor. A maid brought in a tray with a small ceramic coffee pot and set it next to Mrs. Isaac. She poured drinks for the guests who sat at the table. Isaac was gracious attempting to draw his guests into conversation. His wife did not join in and remained seated with the maid at the side of the room, refilling coffee and tea when needed. The coffee was smooth and not bitter.

Isaac was enjoying talking to Zeleka. They conversed in the easy manner of men and women in the Western world. Isaac's wife, although very pretty and becoming in her native garb, had no intellectual pretensions or knowledge of Western customs. She focused on serving the guests food and drink.

Isaac asked Zeleka, "Your project is to evaluate delivery of health care in Ethiopia? Are you getting out in the field and visiting the villages?"

"My specific project is to determine how the villagers are accepting the HIV medications—"

Isaac interrupted. "They're ignorant, not much to evaluate."

Isaac displayed the common prejudice of the educated class of Ethiopians. In their minds, it was useless to expect the rural peoples to grasp anything about HIV. Caanen encountered this approach on a daily basis in the clinic where the younger doctors often spoke in English in front of the patients, stating, "These people are ignorant!"

Later, Caanen joined Zeleka in a taxi and drove back into the city.

"It made me uncomfortable that his wife did not join in with us," said Zeleka.

"I know what you mean. He's a good soul, though. He's had a good education, and with his skills, he could make a big difference around here," said Caanen.

"I think being a doctor here would be so exciting, so gratifying," said Zeleka.

"It certainly makes me feel better about myself trying to help out here," said Caanen.

Zeleka leaned back in the seat, smiled, and nodded toward Caanen and then stared out the window.

DANCE LESSONS

Later that week, Caanen arrived at the pension around eight o'clock in the evening. It was dark, and Floyd's lights were on. Drum music boomed from his open window—a simple, repetitive beat. Caanen felt like company. He knocked on the door.

"Yeah," Floyd said, looking a little startled upon finding Caanen at the door. "Come in."

Caanen walked into the smoke-filled room. Benjamin and Zirro were dancing near the bed. The CD player was at full volume. Benjamin's head was jerking up and down in a rhythmic fashion, violently and rapidly. Zirro sat down on the bed.

"The boys have been teaching me how to dance Tigray fashion. I'm a slow learner," said Floyd. He removed a handkerchief from his trouser pocket and wiped the perspiration from his face. He lit another cigarette. Zirro took one from the package and lit it from the burning end of Floyd's cigarette. Floyd began to lurch up and down and jerk his head forward and backward rhythmically.

This was a major turnabout for Floyd, who had been raised in a very strict and conservative Mennonite household. The Brethren had never really warmed to his lifestyle, and he had moved away from home to escape all their rules and regulations.

Caanen watched the three dancers. They were perspiring profusely.

"We went to Rodeo Restaurant this evening and had rice and lamb and then went over to the bar for a while,' Floyd said.

"Yes, Dr. Robert. Floyd, he really like us a lot. He's going to send us to school when he leaves. Aren't you, Floyd?"

"Sure," Floyd said, locking his arm into that of Zirro and twirling him around the room.

A cell phone rang. Floyd ran his fingers through his graying hair and picked up the phone.

"Yes? Well, I'm busy tonight. Maybe tomorrow." Floyd switched off his phone. "That was Mohammed. He is always waiting for me to come back to my room—it is an ambush, really—to get me to pay some money for his education. It's driving me crazy!"

Benjamin responded with, "That's wrong! That boy should leave you alone!"

"I'll see you tomorrow, Floyd," Caanen said as he closed Floyd's door behind him.

"Good night, Dr. Robert," Zirro and Benjamin said in unison, blowing smoke toward the ceiling.

ROOM NUMBER 46

D r. Mulugeta, the head nurse, and the usual crowd of young nursing students, dressed in crisp, white cotton blouses and dark-blue skirts, were working their way through the ward rooms. The last room, number 46, was on the opposite side of the hall from an eight-bed wardroom. Caanen had never entered the room before.

"What's over here, Mulugeta?" Caanen asked as they eased themselves through the partially opened door.

"This patient has TB. Bad case, failing therapy many, many times, now," said Mulugeta.

Caanen could see through the patient's window out into the quadrangle between the hospital wings. The grass was chest high, and crimson red calla lilies bloomed between drying bedsheets on makeshift clotheslines. The patient's room had the usual rancid odor of soured perspiration. The husband and two children were sitting on the empty bed facing the patient who lay in a coma, spittle dried on her cheeks and on the bedsheets. The mucous that she coughed up was flecked with blood.

"She has TB peritonitis too," Mulugeta said.

Caanen felt the ascites and the doughy consistency of the abdomen.

"You know this is really dangerous, Mulugeta. She likely has highly resistant TB, and we are here without masks," Caanen said.

"Don't worry. I never get TB. Not in thirty years," said Mulugeta.

Caanen left rounds and walked to the clinic. Abdul greeted him and gestured at the line of families waiting to see them. Many families were there with small children, two to eight years of age. Abdul was busy writing demographic data on the charts. Often, only the mother was present. Fathers often disowned their HIV-positive wives and children, although they were the ones who had introduced HIV into the family.

Abdul had little time to spend explaining the disease. It was enough to enroll the child and write prescriptions for antiretroviral drugs. The mother and child walked over to the pharmacy window to get their pills. The line for Abdul had grown to more than fifty people by noon. Caanen was apprehensive about the fact that no patient teaching was taking place, only handing out pills. He wondered how many of these women would be able to give the drugs each day to the children without having received any teaching about the disease and how to treat it.

Zeleka came into the room smiling. She was dressed discreetly, her shoulders covered by a red *shamma*. Abdul looked up, clearly taken by the exotic visitor. She spoke some broken Amharic. The patients responded with smiles. The three saw patients for another two hours.

Later, Abdul suggested, "Let's go for a coffee."

The three walked out to the café and sat down. A corrugated iron roof blocked out the sun. The waitress brought a *buna* for each of them. Abdul put three cubes of sugar into his demitasse cup.

Zeleka turned toward Abdul. "How do you like the clinic?" she asked.

"It's okay. The pay is poor. For now, okay though," he said.

"Did you sign up for this hospital?"

"No, the government assigned me. There's no choice," said Abdul, grimacing.

Zeleka enjoyed being the only Western woman in the hospital. She knew only a little Amharic, but all the doctors were conversant in English. She enjoyed a notoriety that did not exist back in the office in Addis Ababa. That evening, Zeleka joined Caanen and Floyd for dinner at Aytegeb. She wanted the two men's opinions on whether she would make a good doctor. Being a doctor seemed a lot more exciting than being a pencil pusher back at the home office.

MARKET DAY

Caanen and Floyd left the pension late one morning. The walk to Hotel Ghion would be slower than usual, because it was market day. It was cool, and they wore jackets, but the sun was already up, the morning was clear, and no clouds obscured Mount Tossa. Shepherds walked behind their flocks as they made their way up the side of the mountain. A young boy was having a bowel movement in the middle of the road. To their right-hand side was an ornate communal fountain with fat-tailed sheep drinking from a trough fenced off from the spigots that provided water for humans.

The two walked past the secondary school. Teenagers were running to arrive on time. The loudspeaker in the school lot played Frank Sinatra singing "My Way.'" The song served notice that class would begin in several minutes. Consequently, during school week, Caanen and Floyd were always accompanied on their walk by Sinatra. The two men continued making their way up the steep incline past the local mosque, rendered invisible from the road by a wall of enormous blue gum eucalyptus.

They turned onto the main road, which led past an old palace of Hailie Selassie, now dilapidated, the perimeter of chain-link fence lying on the ground. There was a crush of men and livestock. Muslim and Christian farmers alike were herding humpbacked cattle to the city market. Large flocks of fat-tailed sheep dashed across the roadway, pulling at shocks of grass alongside the right-of-way. There was the usual daily traffic of donkeys with their yellow plastic containers filled with cooking oil. Most of the donkeys were without human guides. They traveled their lonely routes from the cooking oil outlet in town to their master's homes laden with vitamin A-fortified cooking oil.

Caanen and Floyd had to step aside sharply on several occasions to avoid being gored by the cattle. The farmers waved their crooks and smiled at them.

Homeowners came out to the road to bargain with the shepherds for one of their flock. After the purchase, the sheep was grasped by a hind leg and frog-walked home by the new owner to be butchered the same day.

Ali greeted Caanen and Floyd in his tattered tuxedo in the foyer of the Hotel Ghion. "How are you, sirs?"

"We're fine, Ali. Usual breakfast for us," Floyd said.

Floyd paid for the meals. When they were done, they walked out onto the road where a steep hillside led down to the hospital from the hotel. Each morning sleeping men were found alongside the tarmac. One man in particular was easily recognizable, because he slept with his bare feet sticking out from under a moldy blanket. His head, however, was covered. Caanen gave some thought to tickling his feet and then thought better of it.

"No way. Don't do that!" said Floyd emphatically.

They walked to the clinic and approached the hospital entrance. Standing mutely at the entrance arch was a tall, powerful man in bare feet and stark-naked. His hair was dirty and matted. His wild look was enhanced by a wide-eyed stare. There were several palm-sized areas on his trunk and buttocks that lacked pigmentation, giving him a piebald look. The two men saluted the guards at the front gate and made for the administration building. The naked man turned and watched them disappear.

"You'll run into that guy quite a lot, just like the girl from the other day," Floyd said.

"I was approached by a gentleman in Addis Ababa by the name of Mr. Million shortly after I arrived. I'm ashamed to say that I did not believe him," said Caanen. "He was trying to enlist my help to clothe a number of insane people who attended a school he started. I thought it was all a scam."

Children with their mothers were waiting to see Abdul. Many of them had severe ringworm of the scalp. The mothers from the Afar region had extensive tattoos from the jaw to the neckline, done in delicate blue tracings. The usual pattern was a stairstep with broad curves at the angle of the jaw to extend the tesselations down the throat.

"Tell her that her tattoos are very charming," Caanen said to Abdul, taken by the exotica.

Abdul spoke to the woman. She reacted bashfully by pulling her headscarf around her face.

The clinic waiting area had a corrugated iron roof that provided shade from the sun and rain. The ground was uneven and rocky. After receiving pills from the pharmacy, the patients removed the bottles from the packing and threw the paper cartons and cotton plugs onto the ground. Caanen made a great show of picking up the paper and sweeping out the pharmacy. Everyone gestured for him to stop. There was too much dust. Caanen spoke to the cleaning ladies with their worn brooms, dust pans, and large sacks and asked them to come to the clinic to remove the trash each morning.

Caanen and Floyd were eager to landscape the waiting room of the clinic. They waited under the roof for the arrival of the hospital maintenance foreman. He eventually arrived with eight young men toting shovels and picks.

"They show up," the foreman said, gesturing to the men. "They work all day, eighty birr. What you want them do?"

"I want them to level the ground under the roof and move all of these boulders. Then I want to put some benches here for the patients to sit on," Caanen said.

The workers shed their shirts and began removing large pieces of turf and pushing boulders to the side.

THE KIDNAPPING

Caanen and Floyd decided to go to Kombolcha to swim. They left the bus station in central Dessie early in the morning. The ride was uneventful for the first hour. As the bus came into sight of Kombolcha, the driver brought the vehicle to a sudden halt. Men with rifles slung on their backs blocked the roadway. A tall, bearded man in a dirty white turban boarded the bus. A heated discussion in Amharic took place between the driver and the armed man. Caanen and Floyd were more puzzled than worried.

The armed man shouted at the driver and passengers to leave the bus, and they gathered into a group by the side of the road. The armed bystanders gathered around the passengers. The bus driver drove off. Minibus traffic continued unimpeded, passing the group on the road. Suddenly, men grabbed the arms of Caanen, Floyd, and an Ethiopian man and forced them to walk down a trail by the side of the roadway. The other passengers fled.

Floyd turned to the Ethiopian who was dressed in clean khaki trousers and a blue blazer over an ironed white shirt. "What's going on?"

"Not sure. Do what they say," he said.

It was clear from the demeanor of the leader that he meant business.

"Are they *shifta*?" asked Caanen.

"No, not robbers," said the Ethiopian.

Caanen looked carefully at the armed men. They appeared to be in their late twenties and early thirties. They had beards, some dyed red. All of them had dirty white *shammas* flung over their shoulders. Several carried AK-47s; the stocks were weather-beaten from years of use, and some of the rifle barrels were rusted. They had green-brown-colored khaki trousers, identical to those worn by the Ethiopian military. Their trouser legs were soiled and tattered. Most of the men had large curved daggers strapped to their waists. The captive Ethiopian who spoke a little English did not appear to be afraid. This reassured the Americans.

An hour later, the group reached a small pond. The captors cupped their hands and drank. Floyd and Caanen refused to drink the water even though their thirst was building. The sun was directly overhead. For the past half hour, they had been trekking almost straight uphill. Caanen could see patches of tilled land intermixed with plots of lime-green millet on the mountainside in front of him. This colorful patchwork of land was one of the many visual treasures of the Highlands. No villages were in sight.

The leader spoke to the Ethiopian prisoner.

"He say we have much more walking," their companion said to Floyd and Caanen. "Drink water!"

Floyd and Caanen stooped and drank the dark water from their hands. Caanen did not tell Floyd the many consequences they could face by drinking contaminated water.

Caanen moved off the trail to urinate. One of the guards placed the barrel of a rifle against the base of his skull. Caanen carefully stopped, his arms akimbo. He turned and looked at the man who gestured to Caanen to get back on the trail.

Late in the day, they stopped on the summit of a mountain. A thatched-roof village was close by. Villagers watched the procession as it passed. They manifested little interest in the group with its two captive Caucasians. The leader stopped downhill of the village. Everyone lay down on the ground. Floyd and Caanen followed suit, only too happy to gain a respite from the arduous trek.

"Maybe this evening we can sneak away," said Floyd.

Their companion looked horrified. "No," he said. "They will kill me if you leave. Maybe they tell us what they want later."

Later, a villager brought a large pot of rice mixed with lamb. Another villager brought a dirty bowl with water. The leader of the group motioned to Caanen and Floyd to join them. The water was brown with gritty sediment. Caanen swallowed the liquid nonetheless, passing the bowl on to Floyd who did the same.

Their companion said to them, "We stay here tonight."

All three captives were unable to sleep because of the cold. One guard was awake all night. At daybreak, a villager came toward the group with a smoldering torch. He talked with the leader, who then gestured with his rifle to Caanen and Floyd to follow the torchbearer. Their fellow captive who acted as the translator stayed behind.

"Just follow. They going to leave you now." With halting English, the man explained that the armed men thought the two Americans were someone else, Germans apparently, and they were going to abandon them.

Floyd and Caanen followed the man to a large tree. The gang leader stood leveling the rifle barrel at the two of them. The other man placed the torch down on the bare ground and grasped a rope wrapped around the tree trunk. He began to lower a four-foot-long cylindrical beehive. The cylinder was plugged with dried earth at each end. Sentinel bees began to swarm out of the hive as it was lowered. Floyd and Caanen began to sidle away from the hive. The gang leader fired a shot into the air and gestured toward the two to get closer and sit down. Caanen was stung on the back of the hands and face. Floyd began shrieking, got on his feet, and danced up and down. Moments later, the two looked up to find the gang leader gone and a honey man waving the smoking torch around the hive, preparing to reach in and extract the combs.

Caanen and Floyd seized that moment to escape. Caanen looked like a tomato, and Floyd was writhing in pain from the stings.

"I'd rather they had just tortured us with whips or knives," said Floyd.

"They gave up on their original plan," said Caanen. "I wonder who they really wanted."

They reached a paved roadway thirty minutes later, after difficult walking. The first vehicle they encountered was a white Land Rover.

Two women from Save the Children Foundation were in the vehicle. Caanen and Floyd waved their arms and stepped out into the path of the car. The driver stopped the car, and the two men got into the back of the Land Rover, which was crowded with wicker baskets. The men explained what had happened to them.

"We live in Dessie," the woman driver said. "We'll take you to the police station at Ge'ez where you can report this."

POLICE STATION

Caanen looked up at the heavy-jowled police captain. Unlike the majority of Ethiopians, this man tended toward the obese side. His blue saucer cap was pushed back on his balding scalp.

"It was mistaken identity," he said. "The gang mistook the two of you for some Germans staying here in Dessie. They wanted to extort money from the German engineering firm that hired them."

"Do you think we're safe staying here longer?" asked Floyd.

"Yeah, they just made a mistake."

"What about the Germans?"

"I'll talk to them."

"Are you going to arrest this group?"

"Impossible. We would be shot trying to take them out of their villages," said the captain, lighting a cigarette.

Caanen looked around at the office with its barren concrete floor, peeling orange paint on the walls, and old metal desk with a rickety swivel chair. There appeared to be no modern features of policing—no phones, no computers, no maps, and no weapons. Caanen felt deflated.

"Let's go, Floyd. This is going nowhere," moaned Caanen.

The two walked out into the quadrangle. The walls were whitewashed and stained waist high with mildew. The grass was uncut, and sheep rustled through the yard. Several lean, brownish-yellow bitches approached them for handouts, their dugs dragging in the pathway. A young police officer, lean and sharp in tailored trousers, passed them, swatting a wooden club against his thigh.

Caanen stopped and looked around. Even in the center of Dessie the land was sere. Mouse birds alighted on a nearby flowering shrub. A hornbill called and flew to the top of a eucalyptus tree. Caanen smiled at the mouse birds hanging upside down from the tree limbs like bagworms. Things did not seem so forlorn and hopeless in the presence of these silly-looking birds.

PASTA AND SAUCE

Caanen took a minibus to the bus stop across from Aytegeb Restaurant. He paid the ten-year-old conductor seventy-five cents and crossed the main street with its cloud of dust and diesel fumes. The factotum at Aytegeb Restaurant was standing by his street-bed with broom in hand, scratching at his neck. He smiled at Caanen. His bed was a corrugated iron box six feet in length, two feet wide, and two feet tall—a coffin-like structure with the foot portion lower than the head. It had legs that held it off the ground. It stood off to the side of the restaurant entrance. Louse-infested bedding draped onto the ground from the foot of the bed. These sleeping quarters were found at all the larger businesses for the guards and workers. Caanen returned the smile and entered the main dining room.

He sat near a window and looked out onto an adjacent empty lot and the main street. He watched the street vendors gather in the lot in the late afternoon. Several women had thrown their blankets onto the ground and were carefully sorting fruit and potatoes, throwing the spoiled objects onto to a heap. A young boy brought a handful of freshly cut grass to a tethered bull. The animal was well fed and strong with a powerful black head and thick scimitar-shaped horns. A man disembarked from the bus, walked into the empty lot, and urinated onto the trash heap.

Caanen finished his macchiato and walked to the Internet shop. He saw Monkey Paws farther up the main street standing outside a furniture shop. The two waved to one another. Caanen sat before the computer and opened his mailbox. The only emails were from Z. Million. He opened one. It read: "Dear Mr. Caanen, Please, if you can, send money for a good project. God will bless you." Caanen sighed, slumped in his chair, and deleted the message. Now, he was a believer, but there was no way to get funds to Mr. Million. He eventually logged out and walked up the hill to the Hotel Ghion to have dinner.

Ali greeted him at the door and showed him into the dining room. The room looked as if it were in perpetual dusk due to the low-wattage lightbulbs. There were no other diners. There had been no conferences at the hotel in the past week and only a handful of hotel guests.

"Pasta and sauce, Ali. Please."

"Lamb?" Ali asked.

"No lamb. Bring me a bottle of Dukum." This was the one meal that Caanen tolerated day in and day out. He was convinced the sweet wine was prophylactic against diarrhea.

Around eight o'clock in the evening, Caanen walked back to the pension. The traffic was light. There was an occasional bus that plied the roadway.

Monkey Paws came up to Caanen out of the darkness. He grinned and held out his hand, palm up. Caanen gave him several birr and gestured for him to buy a new T-shirt.

A light rain began to fall. When Caanen arrived back at the pension, his room was cold. He got undressed and pulled the blankets over himself and fell asleep.

A SINISTER INCIDENT

Caanen awoke to a beautiful, clear, sunny morning. The air had been warming for the past several days. He and Floyd walked to the Hotel Ghion for breakfast. It was their first meal together since the kidnapping. Floyd's appetite was undiminished, whereas Caanen was still ruminating over the meaning of the recent violence.

"Floyd, what the hell are we doing here if we end up getting kidnapped like we did? I thought we were here to be helpful, and I think we are, but no one really seems to give a shit about us," said Caanen.

"Well, I don't think it's all that meaningful as you would put it. We were in the wrong place and got mixed up with someone else. It could happen in New York City for that matter. Besides, it's not our patients who are doing this. Let's just focus on the HIV patients and forget all of this."

The two men walked to the hospital where Dr. Mulugeta was anxious to start rounds. All of the hospital beds had been filled the day before. He was hoping to discharge some of the patients. He and Caanen entered a room filled with young women. Three of them had AIDS. One woman had a severe headache.

"How about you do the spinal tap?" Mulugeta asked.

"Okay," Caanen said. He cleansed the area on the patient's back with iodine. The patient was lying on her right side on the wire bed. Caanen was uncomfortable bending down on his knees and trying to line up the needle. Perspiration dripped from his forehead. The nursing students watched.

Mulugeta gave directions, and Caanen followed his advice. The procedure was given up. He could not hit the lumbar sac.

"It's okay. Try this patient," Mulugeta said.

Again, no luck. Caanen rose from a crouching position and handed the needle to Mulugeta. Mulugeta shuffled to the side of the bed and comfortably bent over and inserted the needle in the patient's back. Clear fluid began to drain from the hub. Mulugeta collected the cerebral spinal fluid and gave it to the nurse.

Later, the two stood over a young woman with tuberculous peritonitis when Wondersson burst into the room.

"Dr. Robert, Dr. Robert, I need your help," Wondersson shouted.

Caanen accompanied Wondersson to the emergency room. The waiting room held one hundred patients, some sitting and others milling about. The adjoining examination room had four beds with patients sitting on each of them. Wondersson led Caanen to a bed with a young girl in her teens sitting on the bedsprings with her gown pulled up to her waist. Blood was oozing from a puncture wound in the middle of her right thigh. She stared at the two doctors.

"This girl was walking down the street near the hospital when some boys ran up to her, stabbed her with a needle, and yelled, 'You have HIV now.' Then they ran away. We have gangs like this in Dessie. They have needles with HIV blood in them and attack people," said Wondersson.

"Did you tell the police?" Caanen asked.

"No. She does not know who the boys are. Should we give medicines?" asked Wondersson.

"There is little choice here. Put her on drugs for a month," said Caanen.

Caanen looked out through the open doors of the emergency room onto the front lawn of the hospital. A large blue-gum eucalyptus tree rose seventy-five feet into the air. Patients were streaming down the footpaths through the yard to the hospital. Five or six thick-billed ravens called to one another from the branches of the tree. One swooped down to retrieve a morsel of food dropped by a patient. The large white patch on the nape of the black neck caught Caanen's attention. Their nasal quacking noises belied their large size and power. They were very social and playful birds that were a welcome distraction from the human antics.

GISHEN

....

Floyd called outside Caanen's room early one Saturday morning. "Are you going to Gishen with us?"

"Yes, just a moment," said Caanen.

Zirro and Benjamin and four hospital employees came to the pension at sunrise. Floyd had arranged for a vehicle to take the group to Gishen. They would take part in an annual pilgrimage to this holy site where a fragment of the Christ's cross was secreted inside the cathedral of Gishen Mariam. Buses had been rendezvousing in Dessie for days, the last staging site for Gishen. They came from hundreds of miles around. Now more than a thousand buses of all makes and sizes lined the roadway, all pointed in the direction of the shrine. The passengers slept aboard the vehicles at night. The drivers started their engines at daybreak, and the racket had awakened Caanen.

Floyd was busy throwing camping gear onto the roof of the truck. The tires on the vehicle were bald. Some of the areas of wear were five to six inches in diameter. One could see the inner tube beneath the wires. The back of the vehicle had a tarpaulin stretched over wooden ribs. Seven grown men were hunched over in the truck bed. Floyd sat down between Zirro and Benjamin.

"Hey, everyone! Listen up! Every group needs a leader, and this is my symbol of authority," shouted Floyd, holding up a large scimitar for all to admire. The knife blade was made of iron, and the entire weapon was twelve inches long. The wooden handle was adorned with numerous rhinestones. Floyd had purchased it the weekend before at a bazaar in town.

The ride to Gishen took eight hours and was excruciatingly uncomfortable. Dust billowed in under the canvas covering. Only Floyd had brought water, and it was used up rapidly. Many vehicles broke down on the roadway, and the pilgrims crowded along the roadside slowly trekking toward the shrine. The cruciform-shaped mountain finally came into sight, and the miles of vehicles began to wend their way up the mountainside. Halfway to the top, the buses began to pull over to the side of the road to park. The truck driver pulled over and shut off the engine. The passengers in the back jumped out and began searching for water. Caanen found some women hawking fruit juices.

A path large enough for only one person had been chiseled out of the mountainside, and the visitors were slowly making their way to the top. At the summit, one entered through an arch to the holy shrine. Floyd walked under the arch just as the sun was setting. He and Zirro hurried to put up a shelter alongside others engaged in the same activity. Floyd's flashlight began to fade. Benjamin and Zirro pulled Floyd down onto their sleeping bags. Floyd placed his prize scimitar beneath his sleeping bag. They ate and joked until exhausted and then fell asleep.

The tolling of the cathedral bells awakened the faithful the following morning. From a loud speaker, the pilgrims were called to the main square in front of the cathedral. Priests in brown and yellow robes and wool knit caps like *tarboshes* led groups of men and women toward the square.

Floyd was aroused by movement below his pillow. He looked among his clothes and cried out, "My knife's been stolen."

"There goes the thief," Zirro shouted, scrambling to his feet.

A bedraggled man limped toward the surging crowd. Several men near him detained him by his arms. Floyd's scimitar was under the culprit's belt, and one man held it aloft and then, with a theatrical flourish, returned it to Floyd. The thief stood stock-still, tears welling in his eyes. The men detaining him dragged him toward the back of an open troop truck. They pulled him up onto the truck bed beneath the canvas. Several members of Floyd's group joined them in the back of the truck. Someone pulled down the back canvas flap. Floyd could not observe what was happening. Bodies lurched against the side of the canvas. There was scuffling in the truck.

"What is going on?" Floyd cried out.

"They're teaching him a lesson," said Zirro.

The canvas flap obscuring the interior of the truck was pulled back, and the men jumped off the truck bed. The thief, now lying on his side, slid out from under the canvas and fell to the ground. His upper lip was split and swollen, and blood oozed from the wound. He was holding his abdomen.

"This is how we deal with thieves," said Zirro.

"God, the knife's not worth beating him up, Zirro. Why don't we call the police?" said Floyd.

"They would treat him worse," said Zirro.

The celebration of the relic of the cross went on for the entire day. Floyd and Caanen found several ladies selling rice and lamb and enjoyed their repast sitting on the ground in the dust and heat surrounded by thousands of worshippers surging backward and forward around the perimeter of the cathedral.

That evening, everyone fell asleep while the sun was still fading. The following morning, they gathered their bedding and stood in line to leave the city gate, one narrow opening that led to a vertical decline down the cliffside. Floyd and Caanen and the boys stood in line for two hours before reaching the portal. The hike to the truck took several more hours.

When they arrived, everyone crawled into the back of the vehicle. Eight hours later, they arrived at Dessie exhausted and coughing from the dust. For at least another week, buses were still stopping alongside the pension with pilgrims disembarking to buy food and water in order to continue their homeward journey.

MOUNT TOSSA

Caanen decided to climb Mount Tossa, a flat-topped mountain known as an *amba,* on the weekend. He laced up his dark-brown Italian leather hiking boots, put several liter bottles of water in his jacket, and left the pension around noon, taking a minibus to the main square. From there, he began the ascent up the mountain. This route was an established roadway decades ago but had fallen into disuse, and the cobblestone was now coarse and almost impassable on foot.

Maria, a malnourished fifteen-year-old HIV-positive patient Caanen had seen at the clinic, came out from one of the hovels not far from the city center and grasped Caanen's hand. They walked a few paces together and then separated. She gestured for him to follow her to her home. He declined her offer by waving to her and the other destitute children surrounding her as he continued up the path.

Caanen was already feeling short of breath. Fifteen minutes more of slow walking, and he turned to survey the city below him. An old palace, now a museum, was perched on a hill surrounded by corrugated iron roofs. There was a strip of buildings along the main road in different states of construction. Some of the newer buildings were several stories high. He was standing above a rural school. An older man in a threadbare polyester suit and flip-flops approached him on the trail.

"Hello," the man said. "You from the States?"

Caanen nodded.

"I'm principal of this school. I teach English also. These are my sons." He waved toward two young boys coming forward while kicking a soccer ball. "I have been here twenty years. I'm very proud of my students. You should go this way." The man gestured to his left at a well-worn path through a dry gulch. "Shortcut to the top."

Caanen continued his trek. Farther up the hill, a band of eight-year-old boys joined him. One very thin boy, whose face was covered by numerous pustules, grabbed Caanen's hand affectionately. He showed his beautiful white teeth. A taller, more mature boy who was clearly leading the group stood looking into Caanen's eyes.

"Birr! I want birr," the tall boy said sneeringly.

"No birr. I have none." Caanen showed his empty palms.

The thin boy grabbed his hand and held it to his chest softly.

The other boys made sounds like a hyena.

"Hyena come!" they screamed in unison.

Caanen feigned fear. They laughed.

The small crowd slowly made its way up the incline. The taller boy separated himself from the rest of the group and began to throw rocks closer and closer to the other boys and Caanen. The group continued up the mountainside. Suddenly, large stones began to tumble from above. The tall boy was standing on top of a large boulder gesturing.

"Bin Laden is coming," he shouted.

The remainder of the boys yelled something to him and signed to Caanen that everything was okay. The boys all turned and left. Caanen was not disappointed. Their young leader was disquieting.

Caanen reached the top of Mount Tossa an hour later. He came upon a shepherd herding fat-tailed sheep on the grassland near the summit. Nearby, a large male gelada baboon slowly and reluctantly led his tribe away from the livestock and over the cliff out of sight. The primate seemed unimpressed by the humans. They were poor adversaries for this animal with his long, sharp fangs and powerful body.

Caanen sat down on a flat rock and looked south toward the Highlands. Mountain ranges and peaks formed an uneven horizon. He could barely make out where a Chinese engineering firm was working on a highway north of Dessie. He turned to walk back, stopping to watch children herd sheep in a valley as it was engulfed with sunlight emerging from behind a cloud.

Off to the right he saw movement. He turned and saw a nyala gently stride through the high grass. The noble turn of its horns was unmistakable—an iconic symbol of Ethiopia.

Caanen began to jog back down the mountain.

FOOT AND MOUTH

Caanen left Hotel Ghion after a breakfast of scrambled eggs, toast, marmalade, and coffee. Like the pasta he ate in the evenings, his breakfast never varied in an unsuccessful attempt to avoid diarrhea. He walked to the hospital. It was sunny and warm, and there was no dust in the air. Many new peddlers' tents were staked out on the main road leading to the hospital. Business was brisk at most of the tents, generally women searching for household items.

Hospital rounds with Mulugeta were routine. They made their way slowly to room number 46. Five or six nursing students, the two physicians, and family members crowded into the room. The woman was a little better; she had been able to eat some rice. Mulugeta ordered the family to take the patient to the shower and bathe her.

As Caanen walked through the crowd around the clinic, a young woman grabbed his sleeve.

"Look!" she said, pointing to her right foot. She had no sandal on the foot. There were several large growths between the third and fourth digits, the size of brussels sprouts, with pus and blood draining around the edges of the lesions.

Caanen went into the clinic and retrieved Abdul. "Ask her how long the lesion has been there," Caanen said.

Abdul talked to the woman who had just learned that she had HIV. The lesion on her foot had been growing for months. Caanen asked the woman to accompany him to see Mulugeta. He handed a water bottle to the patient and motioned for her to clean the foot. There was no soap. The water removed layers of road dirt.

"Mycetoma," Mulugeta said emphatically. "Start some sulfa. Common in people from the Afar region. That is where she is from. I can tell from her dress."

The Afar was a mysterious region. People from the region were exotic, often handsome, haughty, and laconic. Caanen observed the woman's flowing yellow and black garment. She wore a black veil that, however, did not hide the striking tattoo pattern at the angle of the jaw and on her neck. Pewter jewelry shaped into small cups and trumpets hung around her neckline. She had adorned her fingers with numerous silver rings, and henna curlicues darkened her palms.

"That is a disfiguring lesion," said Caanen.

"She is more worried about the sore than the HIV," said Mulugeta. "Start her on sulfas, and it will heal in six months or so."

After lunch, Caanen returned to the clinic. Abdul arrived and opened the clinic doors. The first patient Caanen saw with Abdul was also from the Afar. The man was in his late fifties, six feet tall, and wearing a *shamma* over a robe-like gown that left his legs bare. He had a trimmed beard from ear to ear without a moustache, all of it dyed orange-red. His skin was jet-black. A large scimitar was fastened to his waist by a cloth belt.

"Abdul, why does he dye his beard red?" asked Caanen.

"Many Muslim men from Afar dye their beards," said Abdul. "He has a swelling on his right jaw. It has been there for months. He is taking his HIV medications every day."

Caanen opened the patient's mouth. The skin at the jaw was swollen, red, and hard. "This is lumpy jaw, Abdul. He'll need long-term penicillin."

KOMBOLCHA

T hings were slow in the hospital the following week. Wondersson walked out to the clinic and proposed that everyone make a trip to Kombolcha to go swimming. Kombolcha was forty miles southeast of Dessie and several thousand feet lower in altitude. There, the weather was hot, and the local mosquitoes carried malaria. Wondersson said that Zeleka would be joining the group.

Desarie, Floyd's personal rehabilitation project, was standing nearby and chimed in, "All right! The ladies love me in Kombolcha!" Desarie leered wolfishly for the benefit of Caanen.

Wondersson, Abdul, Floyd, Caanen, Desarie, and Zeleka gathered at the bus station. It was drizzling as they stuffed themselves into an already-crowded robin's-egg-blue Toyota minibus. The windows were closed, and the odor of perspiration and dirty feet was unmistakable. The man sitting next to Caanen carried a plastic bag filled with hides of freshly slaughtered sheep. The odor of liquefied fat added to the stench. Caanen felt a little dizzy from the odors.

The bus lurched out of Dessie and took a slow, broad turn to begin the descent into Kombolcha. A tall, naked man stood by the roadside gesturing at the driver with his shepherd's crook. The driver honked, and the passengers grinned as the mini bus drove onward.

It began to rain as they approached Kombolcha. Brown water rushed across the road in torrents. Branches and stones fell onto the roadway from the adjacent hillside. A large banana tree fell across the roadway just in front of the bus. The driver swerved, almost overturning the bus. They finally arrived in Kombolcha where hundreds of people were waiting in the rain at the bus station to board. There was a subdued yellow glow on the horizon. Abdul led the group to a restaurant on the opposite side of the street. They ducked under an awning and sat down for *buna* and beer.

"It's too cold to swim," said Abdul. "I'm going to get some *khat*."

"I'm with you," said Desarie.

"We're heading to the pool," said Wondersson, hailing a cab.

The four coworkers took the taxi to the municipal pool on the outskirts of the city. A high chain-link fence enclosed a small neighborhood. Soldiers armed with AK-47s stood guard in a tower at the entrance to the compound.

Dressing cubicles with louvered doors lined a hillside above the pool. Caanen entered and changed into his swimming trunks. Zeleka strapped herself into her lime-green bikini top in the next cubicle while smiling at Caanen. Floyd and Wondersson also got into their trunks.

The swimming pool was rectangular, large, and deep with beach chairs scattered around. Caanen dove in and felt the contrast of the soothing warm water after the light, cold drizzle that was still falling. He swam laps in the pool. Zeleka dove into the pool, and Wondersson immediately followed her. His swimming skills were weak. He swam toward Caanen who suggested that he talk to Zeleka. Perhaps she could help him to swim better.

Floyd eased himself into the pool and enjoyed the tepid water. It was unusual for him to leave the cares of the hospital behind him. He soon got out and stretched out on a reclining chair with the towel draped over his body.

Caanen got out as well and stood poolside to dry off. The grass around the pool was waist high. A bee-eater flitted onto the telephone line at the edge of the compound and began to call. Behind the compound a roaring stream fed by the heavy rainfall could be heard. Caanen returned to his cubicle, dressed, and walked into the street.

A camel caravan passed by, making its way to a crossing upstream from the pool. Caanen watched the animals as they traversed the raging stream, unperturbed by water rising to their chests.

Caanen returned to the compound and entered the coffee bar. A large group of men were gathered in front of a television watching a soccer game. He ordered a macchiato and wandered out onto the patio. Abdul, Desarie, and an unfamiliar young woman were sitting under an umbrella chewing *khat*. Desarie introduced his female acquaintance. Abdul had reached a low after hours of chewing *khat* leaves. Beside him on the ground were branches stripped of all their leaves. Desarie and his girlfriend wandered away from the patio. They began to argue, and the young woman walked briskly away toward the entrance to the compound.

Later, the group took a taxi to the bus station, which was still crowded. People mobbed every minibus that arrived. Each minibus, however, seated only nine adults. Wondersson took charge of Zeleka and left in one bus. Caanen forged his way through the crowd and captured a window seat. The bus started off rapidly. The child conductor took Caanen's fare.

Ten miles outside Kombolcha the minibus began the long climb up the mountain to Dessie. Suddenly, there was an explosion beneath Caanen's seat. It was a blowout. The passengers grabbed their belongings and stepped off of the bus. The driver rolled the spare tire to the back of the bus as the passengers watched. He inspected the tire. The rubber on the spare was denuded to the wire support and lacked air. The sun was setting.

The men stood around smoking, and the women gathered into a tight group. Caanen joined the women, worried about being left alone thirty miles from Dessie. He could see smoke curling from the rooftop of a shanty on a nearby hill. Suddenly, it seemed very lonely. Caanen recalled the prowling hyenas in Dessie and wondered if they were common in this area.

The women started walking uphill. Caanen followed. A large bus came to a stop beside them. Everyone pushed into the center aisle of the bus, and Caanen sat down on a box offered by a female passenger. The bus was overloaded and had trouble negotiating the incline to Dessie. The driver never shifted out of second gear. One headlight was burned out, and the other headlight beamed out over the mountain chasm. The driver carefully negotiated each hairpin turn. They arrived in Dessie four hours later. Caanen was relieved and thanked the bus driver for picking him up and joyfully gave him twenty birr.

LABOR RELATIONS

Several weeks passed. Dr. Mongistu, chief of the clinic, wanted an urgent meeting with Floyd and Caanen. They both arrived at eight o'clock in the morning. Mongistu was in his office. Old calendars in Amharic hung on the walls, coiled into rolls from the humidity.

"Good morning. Please sit down," said Mongistu from behind his desk. He was a tall man in his midthirties, thin and well dressed. He wore an expensive black leather jacket with stylish European lines.

"Remember Mr. Fisk telling us that we should have the employees work weekends?" he said.

Floyd nodded.

"Well, no one has been paid for their work. They're all complaining—the doctors, the nurses, the pharmacists and the lab technicians. I've called to talk to Fisk, but I cannot get a hold of him. Can you help?" said Mongistu.

"That's all we need," said Caanen.

"I'll call Dutton Foundation and straighten this out right now," Floyd replied. He immediately called Evers at the Foundation on his cell phone. "Peter, this is Floyd in Dessie ... Yes, good. Everything is fine except for the eleven people who have not been paid for their work. This has been going on since Fisk was here ... Well, that was the understanding of everyone here. They've had no days off now … Still, someone has to pay them. The wheels are going to come off up here if we don't."

Floyd grimaced and put the cell phone in his pocket.

"He's denying he had anything to do with the request to work. He says it's an issue to take up with Fisk, not him. Shit!" Floyd grimaced through his teeth. Everyone present in the room knew Fisk promised that the AIDS Training Center would foot the bill. Since no one had been paid, it was obvious he was reneging on the deal.

"Let's figure out how much money is owed," said Caanen.

The three men walked to the clinic.

Abdul approached them as they walked up. "Are we going to be paid?" Abdul asked.

The lab technicians joined the crowd. Everyone crowded around.

Caanen said to the group, "Under no circumstances should anyone work another weekend until everyone is paid."

Abdul looked perplexed. "Well, maybe we'll do that, maybe not. The patients will come anyway. They think the clinic is open every day now. I can't desert them."

The lab director chimed in. "This is not right. Already I'm working a second job every evening and then every weekend. Maybe we should all quit."

"We will work this next weekend only. No more weekends after that," Mongistu declared.

Caanen went into the hospital to make morning rounds. Dr. Mulugeta greeted him at his office. He was reading a 1990 edition of the *Merck Manual*, nearly twenty years old and the lone textbook in the entire hospital. Mulugeta was the only physician doing inpatient work. He had no one to share weekends or holidays with. His day began at sunup and ended late each afternoon.

The two men walked to one of the women's wardrooms. Mulugeta placed a needle into the belly of a young woman with HIV and tuberculous peritonitis. She was complaining of pain from the swelling of her abdomen. Amber-colored fluid drained slowly down the tubing into a clear plastic bag lying on the concrete floor.

"Is there a chest X-ray to look at?" asked Caanen.

"Look in her belongings," said Mulugeta.

Caanen went to the head of the patient's bed. There was a rickety metal dresser with a drawer at the top and cupboard below. One dresser leg was shorter than the others, causing it to list to one side. It was battered and chipped. Caanen opened the cupboard to find the X-ray. He moved aside the tin pots containing her rice. He held the X-ray up to the sunlight coming through the window. There were signs of pneumonia in the left lower lobe of the woman's lungs.

"Check to make sure she has her medicines," said Mulugeta.

Caanen opened the drawer and searched through scraps of paper. He found the purchase slip from the hospital pharmacy and boxes of antitubercular medicines. The patient would improve with time and daily medication.

PRISONERS' ADVOCATE

One Sunday afternoon, Caanen relaxed around the pension, reading while sitting in the sun. A new visitor was staying in the guesthouse and was seated on the porch in front of his room. A large, white, brand-new Land Cruiser was parked in the lot. Caanen had noticed the arrival of the vehicle earlier in the day with its well-heeled occupants and was curious to know what NGO they worked for.

"I'm Sebastian with *Medicins Sans Frontieres*," Sebastian replied in English with a slight French accent. "I am trying to find out how many prisoners in the regional jail have HIV."

Sebastian was dressed in blue jeans and a black turtleneck sweater. He had dark curly hair worn modishly long. He leaned back against the divan on the porch. He had a small glass of Cointreau in his left hand.

"How do you know who has HIV among the prisoners?" asked Caanen.

"The prison system here is excellent, not like the United States." He glanced sideways at Caanen as he entered data into his laptop as he spoke. "Ethiopia is very compassionate toward prisoners," said Sebastian.

"Not from what I have observed," said Caanen.

"Do you know that at the regional jail in Dessie, 90 percent of the prisoners with HIV are on medications? First-world countries can't give that kind of care."

"Well, we don't have those kind of figures at the clinic," said Caanen, finally realizing that the facts were not the issue with Sebastian. "Where are you from in France?"

"I live in Toulon. We leave tomorrow to inspect the jails in Lalibela and then on to Ankober," said Sebastian.

Leila, the hotel day clerk, came up to Caanen. "You call telephone, this number. They call today, very worried."

Caanen took the piece of paper. "Good luck in Lalibela," said Caanen.

The Frenchman nodded his head and lifted his tumbler in salute.

Caanen started for his room. He used his cell phone to call the number. Evers answered.

"We're not responsible for paying those hospital employees. That's up to Fisk, so don't involve the Foundation," said Evers.

"Well, there's no way you're not involved. Everything that happens is perceived, rightly or wrongly, to come from the Foundation. I'm meeting with Mongistu tomorrow, and I'll pay the folks from my monthly allotment," Caanen retorted.

"Don't involve me any further. I'm in Awash National Park until next week. Testfaye is carrying a cell phone if you can't reach mine," said Evers.

The following morning, Dr. Mongistu approached Floyd and Caanen as they walked into the hospital compound. He had all of the workers who had not been paid with him.

"Any news from Dutton about the pay?" asked Mongistu.

"Yes, it's all taken care of. Let's get you what we owe you," replied Caanen.

The employees smiled as they lined up to be paid.

It rained softly as Caanen returned to the pension from the Hotel Ghion after dinner. It had been a solitary dinner with only Ali and Caanen in the dimly lit dining room.

Caanen got into bed and began reading. He heard the pension guard opening the front gate for a taxi.

There was a soft knock at his door.

"Robert?" said a young woman's voice from behind the door.

Caanen opened the door after pulling on some jeans. It was Zeleka. "Hello," he said.

"Mind if I come in?" she said.

"No. Come in. What's up?" Caanen pulled on a shirt and buttoned it up.

"Can I spend the night?" she asked frankly.

"Is there something wrong?" he asked.

"No. I want to spend the night with you."

"I'm truly flattered, but we would have hell to pay in the end. Besides, I am too old for you. It's too late for you to go home. Here, you take my bed. I'll take the chair," he said.

The following morning, Floyd knocked on the door and entered. Caanen was pulling on his clothes as Zeleka was showering.

"Oh, sorry!" Floyd smiled. "I'll come back later."

"No, wait a minute, Floyd. Zeleka is in there showering. Let's go to breakfast now!"

SISTERS OF CHARITY

Isaac arrived that morning at the clinic.

"Dr. Robert, maybe you can come with me this morning. I'm going to visit some workers for Save the Children Foundation."

The two walked up the steep incline from the hospital entrance to the main thoroughfare.

"This way." Isaac gestured to his right. "You can see the top of the house just over there."

Caanen looked at the oversized structure rising among the hovels surrounding it.

"This was my home, but I rented out to two women from the States."

They walked to the front door and rang the doorbell. A woman in blue jeans and a T-shirt answered the door. Her hair was short, and she appeared preoccupied and then startled.

"Dr. Isaac! And Dr. Caanen! Come in, please. Jean, come and join us," she shouted into the hallway of the house. "Please come on in, both of you! We already know Dr. Caanen," she said, explaining herself to Dr. Isaac. Caanen suddenly recognized her as one of the women in Land Rover who had picked up Floyd and him on the highway after being kidnapped.

"We know each other," he said to Isaac. "She picked Floyd and me up not long ago—we were puffed up with bee stings."

The three were joined by Jean, a thin, dark, serious-appearing woman with black-rimmed glasses. The group went into the living room with its large windows overlooking the corrugated iron rooftops. The new mosque built with Saudi money was visible on a distant hilltop.

Isaac looked at the mosque. "It makes me angry they're building all of these mosques in Ethiopia with foreign money. The Muslims are not helping us, and they're just about everywhere. We have a joke in Ethiopia. Mohammed is the most common name in our country, so someone can just shout out the name Mohammed and someone will come running."

He went on to talk about the disorder among the Muslim community near Kombolcha. Several British tourists had been harassed since the episode involving Floyd and Caanen. "There is no way to know what is really going on around here," said Isaac. "When was the last time you saw a newspaper?"

Caanen looked around the room with its collection of antique basketware and textiles fastened to the walls. Large photo albums graced the coffee table in front of the women.

"Things have slowed down for us," said Jean. "We have placed most of the orphans we had in local settings, and Barbara and I are thinking of taking a collecting trip for a month. I want to get some Oromo baskets."

Isaac and Caanen stayed for coffee, and the two aid workers showed them the trinkets they had collected in their two years in Dessie. They offered to drive the men over to the hospital. Dr. Isaac declined the offer. The two men began walking back toward the hospital alongside the street side bazaar.

"My family was very prominent in Dessie," noted Isaac. "The motel you are staying in was my mother's house. It was taken away from her by the Derg. This house, I built ten years ago, but it provides more income for me to rent it."

Isaac suddenly stopped walking and bowed graciously to a middle-aged woman dressed in a saffron-colored silk robe with a similarly colored scarf over her head. Unlike Isaac, she had a nut-brown color to her skin. Her face was full and kindly. He introduced the woman to Caanen.

"This is one of my sisters," Isaac said. "She is married to a man who had a grocery store near here, but the Derg took it away from him. They are poor people now."

Caanen continued walking back to the pension. He saw Monkey Paws skipping alongside the main roadway, whacking the fence palings in front of Aytegeb Restaurant with a stick. The road crew was applying the finishing touches to the fence. The metal piping used to make the fence was painted a chalky blue. Caanen was disappointed to see that the retaining fence was put up so haphazardly. The posts were not straight, and the horizontal bars were not level. This was a frequent outcome with the stunning lack of craftsmanship among the male urban population. Besides the hospital, which was built years ago during Selassie's reign, there were very few pleasing buildings in the entire city.

RED RIBBONS

aanen resumed his normal work week. There was no electricity at the hospital the next day. A meeting of all clinic personnel took place at one o'clock in a building next to the HIV clinic. Caanen waited on the top step, listening to the ravens arguing in a eucalyptus. The doctors and nurses began to arrive in groups of two and three. Once everyone was assembled, Floyd opened the meeting. He eventually got around to the message he wanted to leave with the clinic workers.

"We're not doing enough to teach patients about the disease they are living with. We're giving them medications and expecting them to take them for the remainder of their lives without any explanation of why."

"In the long run, this is going to lead to failure," said Caanen.

Caanen talked about poor record keeping and the fact that records were misfiled or lost. The discussion continued for an hour.

"There's too much emphasis on starting patients on medications," Floyd added.

Dr. Mongistu stood up and disagreed. He quoted Dutton's mandate. "Put as many people as possible on drugs, especially children."

At that point, Floyd stood up and asked everyone to stand and hold hands.

"We're going to stand here quietly for a minute and think about those of us who have passed away from this disease. Now, try and remember their faces."

Everyone stood by awkwardly.

Floyd took a small branch that was fastened to an old lampstand and placed it in front of him on a table. He began to hang red ribbons on the branches.

"Each one of these ribbons represents a patient in the clinic who has died of AIDS this month."

He handed ribbons out to the others for them to place on a branch. Caanen noticed that one of the nurses had tears on her cheeks. The lamp with its branch was draped with red ribbons. The group filed quietly out into the bright sunshine.

That evening, Caanen went to the Hotel Ghion for his usual dinner. Ali was alone in the reception room. The lounge was empty.

"Hello, sir," said Ali. "You want dinner?"

"Yes," said Caanen. "The usual—pasta and sauce." Caanen had lost fifteen pounds on his monotonous, daily diet of pasta and sauce.

YOU WORK FOR THE FOUNDATION!

A week later, Evers came to Dessie bringing Zeleka with him. He asked to meet with Caanen. He then commandeered Dr. Mongistu's office and sat behind the desk. Caanen walked into the office.

"Hello, Dr. Caanen," Evers said.

Caanen sat down on the dirty couch.

"We have a real problem here," Evers continued. "Our entire role can be defined in simple terms. Our mission is simply to see to it that as many children as possible are put on medications so that we can save the future of this country. This was Dutton's wish. There was no reason for you to get involved in the pay of the clinic workers. We need them working every weekend. I don't want to interrupt starting kids on medicine. So, I don't want you changing the workers' focus here." Evers tapped his hand on the desktop.

Caanen stared at the young man. "Your goal is laudable. It's getting there that is the problem. The emphasis on quantity is not going to provide the answer to this problem. We need to teach the people about their illness, not just hand out pills. They need to understand why they cannot miss a pill. There is simply nothing like that happening now. I'd be remiss if I didn't make you aware of this."

"You've told me all this before," Evers said, exasperated.

"You need to address the problem from the perspective of total health care—adults, children, pregnant mothers, and so on. We're starting children on medications in the clinic, and at the very same time, HIV-positive mothers are delivering infected babies in the hospital. We're handing out medicines at the front door, while more infections are coming through the back door."

"I'm aware of it, and I can see that we are not on the same page. I appreciate the time you have put in," Evers said disingenuously. "I will call Dutton when I get back to Addis and see what his plans are on proceeding from here. There is another issue here too. I don't like your relationship with Zeleka."

Caanen looked dumbfounded. "What relationship are you talking about? The Foundation is your business, Peter. Zeleka's relationships are not. At least not that I am aware of," Caanen said.

Evers had a pained expression on his face. He got up and walked away.

Later that afternoon, Zeleka and Caanen walked to the hospital coffee shop. Each had a *buna*. Caanen mixed in two lumps of sugar. He watched several kites soaring above them. Nearby was a kiosk used by the immigration service to vaccinate Ethiopians prior to them leaving for Qatar and other Middle Eastern states to become maids and butlers.

"So, how are things in Addis?" asked Caanen.

"Not very exciting," said Zeleka. "I wish I could stay here and work, but Evers doesn't think it's safe for a woman here. I think he's getting a little too possessive."

I'M NOT GAY

Floyd and Caanen were now familiar faces each morning along the road to the Hotel Ghion. Caanen observed one older man for several weeks creating a space on the road where he made mud to apply to the wattled walls of several outbuildings. He began by forming a semicircle barrier of rocks placed on the roadway and overlaid the roadway with straw. Each day he added cattle manure, clay, new straw, and water. The mix fermented for several weeks with daily layers of manure and straw being added. The previous week, Caanen had noticed the man stomping in the liquid mud in his bare feet. Today, an entire crew of young men arrived and were helping the man plaster the outside of two large sheds and a house.

Abdul met Caanen at the front door of the clinic and introduced him to a young man in a dark-blue serge suit, white shirt, and highly shined light-brown shoes.

"This is Mohammed. He's come from Addis to see if you can tell him if he is doing okay," Abdul said. His last CD4 count was twenty-five, and he is taking all of his medicines. He has some sores on his back that will not go away. He wants you to look at them."

Mohammed and Caanen walked into the clinic and pulled the curtain across the cubicle. Mohammed had lined his eyes with henna, and his beard was impeccably shaven. He loosened his belt, lowered his trousers, bent over the exam table, and pulled down his underwear. Large ulcers with clear discharge ringed his anus. Some of the ulcers were so deep that Caanen could place his gloved forefinger to the depth of his knuckle.

"Abdul, ask him how long these have been present," Caanen said to Abdul.

"He says for months."

"I want him to take this medicine for herpes and come back in a week and see if things improve," Caanen said.

Caanen explained to Abdul that the lesions were herpes ulcers often seen in gay men with advanced AIDS back in the 1980s in the United States. In Ethiopia, homosexuality was unlawful and subject to a death sentence. The topic was *verboten* in the clinic.

"I asked him if he was gay, but he said no," said Abdul.

KITFO

Caanen wandered over to the laboratory. Two technologists were looking through the microscope at fresh stool specimens from patients with diarrhea, a very common complaint. Diarrhea led to hospitalization of several adults a week, an unheard of problem in Western hospitals. One out of five stool studies ordered had parasites, either amoebae, eggs, or worms. Caanen returned to the clinic and wrote out some scripts. Dr. Mongistu, Desarie, and Abdul were waiting to leave with Floyd for lunch.

"Come with us," said Desarie. He was two hours late for work and looked hungover.

The group went to Lalibela Restaurant. Caanen insisted on ordering sautéed vegetables with rice. Abdul and Desarie ordered *kitfo*, raw beef served with a *berbera*, or red sauce. Mongistu ordered a pizza.

"After caring for people with diarrhea every day, I don't know how the two of you could eat *kitfo*," Caanen said to Abdul and Desarie.

Desarie theatrically ogled the raw meat and reached for some with a handful of *injera*. Abdul ordered *tej*, a honey wine with the odor and taste of beeswax.

"It's a good practice to drink alcohol with *kitfo*, because it helps kill the parasites," said Abdul. "About once a month I take an antiparasitic drug too, just to make sure I am okay."

"I will pass on the *kitfo*," said Caanen.

Desarie leaned back from the low table, stuffed some *injera* and *kitfo* in his mouth, and then reached for his package of cigarettes.

The group decided to walk back to the clinic. They were overtaken every few minutes by speeding NGO Land Cruisers raising clouds of dust that choked the pedestrians. Caanen felt the ire rising within him toward these privileged drivers and their passengers. They drove at breakneck speed in spite of the children and donkeys clogging the streets.

Dr. Mongistu said to Abdul and Caanen, "You are going to be short in the clinic from now on."

"'Why? What now?" asked Caanen.

"The pediatrician who was to start Monday in the clinic has disappeared," Mongistu said.

"'Great!" said Abdul.

"I don't understand," said Caanen.

"He just packed his bags and left for Addis yesterday," said Mongistu. "That's what his friends told me."

That evening, Caanen walked to the city center with Floyd. The storefronts were thrown wide open, and polyglot music at the highest decibel level blared toward the strollers. They had a macchiato at Aytegeb and watched television. Skirmishes of Ethiopian soldiers with revolutionaries near Somalia replaced the daily diet of floods on the television set. The Ethiopians evinced no interest in the broadcasts. Soon the Meskel ceremony would begin. Floyd was looking forward to attending the festivities in Dessie stadium.

FINDING THE TRUE CROSS

T he following week there was a great festival. Meskel was an annual event, much looked forward to by Ethiopian Christians. Donkeys, loaded with yellow plastic containers filled with cooking oil, carried out their morning duties oblivious to the festive preparations. Early in the evening, Christians began gathering in the soccer stadium. Floyd was eager to attend the ceremony. He insisted Caanen follow him and stop working on clinic data.

The town square was crowded by four o'clock in the afternoon. Policemen were conducting monks and priests to the front of a long line that wound into the stadium. Children carried bundles of dried twigs to toss onto the pyramid of limbs and trees. All of this would be set ablaze in the ceremony. Tents in the bazaar were selling *addis abebe* to adorn the torches.

Floyd and Caanen got in line with the townsfolk and entered the stadium along with thousands of onlookers. A large, twenty-foot-high wooden cross was assembled in the center of the stadium. Darkness began to descend. The younger folk were delirious in anticipation of setting the stacked timber and cross on fire. The priests took a promenade around the periphery of the stadium, and one tall, bearded man with a yellow cap retrieved a torch from a small fire and tossed it on the pile of bundled tree limbs. Within a minute, flames were shooting one hundred feet into the air. The crowd was shouting and swaying from side to side.

Later, as the crowd dispersed, the police were everywhere on the lookout for pickpockets and thieves. Each carried a truncheon, and every officer was fit and strong. Caanen and Floyd jostled against other pedestrians as everyone began to radiate out from the stadium.

"I've never seen a fire like the one started tonight," said Floyd. "I have a feeling it may be one of the last festivities we will be attending here."

THE CHARITABLE BROTHER

S aturday morning, Caanen walked toward the main doors of the hospital after making quick rounds. Several women stood about with their *shammas* pulled tightly about their head and necks. Their feet were dirty and wet with only fragments of sandals remaining. A light drizzle was falling. He was greeted by Dr. Isaac who had just entered the hospital.

"I'm going to see my maid," Isaac said. "She's having abdominal pain and is in the hospital."

Caanen turned about and accompanied him to one of the large wardrooms. Isaac introduced him to his maid. She had blankets pulled up to her chin. She was in her fifties. She did not speak and lay shivering in the bed. The nurse had just begun intravenous fluids.

Isaac talked to her in Amharic and palpated her abdomen. She winced when he pushed on the right side of her abdomen.

"She's had gallbladder problems before. I think it is the same problem now. I will go and buy some antibiotics and soft foods," Isaac said.

The two men walked to a small store across the street. The waist-high grass along the roadside was wet and dripping. As they were stepping into the store, a deafening crack of thunder followed a lightning strike to a nearby tree. The clerk, Isaac, and Caanen all jumped upward and then grinned at one another. Torrents of rain began to fall. They stood in the store beneath the corrugated iron roof for twenty minutes and waited for the storm to abate. Isaac bought some soft rolls and fruit juice to take to the patient. Finally, when the rain subsided into a light drizzle, the two ran for the hospital. Once inside, Isaac went to the pharmacy and purchased ampicillin for an intravenous injection. He stopped a nurse in the hallway and gave the drug to her and asked her to begin administering the antibiotic.

"My wife does not think that I should spend our money on our maid. She is of the old school, meaning she has no compassion for those outside of our social set. This is still a problem in Ethiopia. Compassion is something that must be taught, particularly for people who are not one of your tribe," said Isaac.

Caanen left Isaac at the entrance to the hospital compound. They shook hands. Isaac started home to return to his wife and child, while Caanen headed off to the pension.

MARCH ORDERS

Dr. Mulugeta met Caanen for rounds in the hospital. His wife and two young sons stood in the hallway. Mulugeta handed his wife birr notes.

"School is starting for them tomorrow," said Mulugeta.

His wife took their sons by the hands and led them down the hallway and out of the hospital. She was wearing a beautiful yellow *shamma*. Mulugeta removed his jacket and put his arms into the sleeves of his threadbare white jacket.

There was a shortage of blankets for the patients. In the women's ward, three new patients, teenage girls, were admitted with gowns only. Although the temperatures were in the eighties during the day, the nighttime temperatures remained chilly, often in the fifties and sixties. Mulugeta convinced the other women in the room to share their blankets with the young girls.

Floyd came up to Mulugeta and Caanen while they were walking in the hall.

"I just got a call from Evers. You're to call him back when you have a moment. He was really unfriendly," Floyd said to Caanen.

The two walked over to the clinic. Caanen used his cell phone to call Evers at the Foundation.

"Evers here."

Caanen explained who was calling.

"I talked to Dutton as I said I would. He wants the organization to go in a different direction, treating children only. I know that you're not a pediatrician, and so I'll understand if you don't want to continue on at the clinic. We're going to provide no direct support to adult patients. The other NGOs will pick up the slack there. We can have a driver down at the end of the week to pick you and Floyd up if you want," Evers said.

"All right," said Caanen.

"See you when you get to Addis," Evers said before hanging up.

"Well, we've received our marching orders, Floyd. They're closing down the adult program. He says they're going entirely to child HIV care. Kind of excludes us, don't ya think? Let's inform Dr. Mongistu of what's happened," said Caanen.

Caanen and Floyd walked toward the surgery clinic door. Off to the side of the door lay the mute, crazy, naked man. He lay in the direct sunlight with his left leg elevated on a small boulder. It was weeping fluid from a massive swelling of the calf. His left hand was shading his face. His one garment lay off to the side with bread crumbs on it. Both of the men paused, stared at him for a moment, and then went to Mongistu's office where they informed him of their upcoming departure.

HARAR

Floyd was keen to see one last exotic site in Ethiopia. He had traveled to Lalibela and seen its churches hewn out of stone. He had also been to Lake Tana, the source of the Nile River. Zirro and Benjamin agreed to accompany him on an excursion to the isolated walled city of Harar. Here again, Caanen wondered about the wisdom of escorting these young men. In spite of their moustaches, they were lithe and epicene. The boys assured Floyd that this strictly Islamic city would welcome him, and the three could stay together in a pension. Floyd was a little skeptical of the accommodations in the city but was game to try. Caanen could not understand the interest in Harar. He knew Floyd did not read poetry, and therefore, it was unlikely he was on a search for areas frequented by Arthur Rimbaud who lived in Harar more than a century earlier.

The three hired a taxi to take them the entire distance. Floyd and Caanen agreed to communicate by phone every other day.

Today, Harar is famed for foolish men who feed hyenas from their mouths in the depths of night, not poets. Floyd planned to take photographs of the hyena men.

Two days later, Caanen received a call on his cell phone while making rounds. Floyd's name appeared on the screen. He stepped out into the hallway of the medical ward.

"Hello, Floyd. What's up?" said Caanen.

"Dr. Robert, this is not Floyd. It is Zirro. Floyd, he is very sick. We took him to the hospital. He has diarrhea."

"Is he in the hospital?"

"Yes. The doctor is supposed to call you today," said Zirro.

Caanen returned to rounds, worried that he could do little to help Floyd. Floyd was more than a day's travel by automobile from Dessie, and there were no airline flights. He informed Mulugeta of Floyd's problem.

"The hospital there is not much good," said Mulugeta. He continued on down the hall in his undulating gait.

That afternoon, Caanen received a call from a physician at the hospital in Harar. He said that Floyd was sick with diarrhea but that they had started intravenous fluids and he should be better by the morning. Caanen rang off.

The next morning, Zirro called again. "Floyd, he much worse," he said. "He's not speaking this morning."

"Can you bring him here, Zirro?"

"No, I think he's too sick. There is no airplane here either. I have doctor to call you soon."

Caanen would need nine hours to return to Addis and then another six hours on the road from Addis to Harar.

The physician called again.

"Mr. Floyd is still in coma. He have lots of watery stools, and his blood pressure is low."

Caanen urged him to begin several antibiotics and lots of fluids. The doctor was firm about the risky nature of transporting Floyd to Addis.

"He die if we move him."

Caanen decided to drive to Harar immediately. He engaged a taxi driver with a vehicle in good condition. The driver was reckless as he sped through the villages with his hand pressed on the horn. They almost struck a donkey. He ran over a green monkey that raced from one side of the road to the other. Caanen remonstrated.

Suddenly, the driver came to a halt alongside some thatched huts. Camels stood about loaded down with large plastic bags of charcoal. After a twenty-minute delay, the driver returned with a small child carrying a sack of charcoal, which the driver loaded onto the top of the taxi.

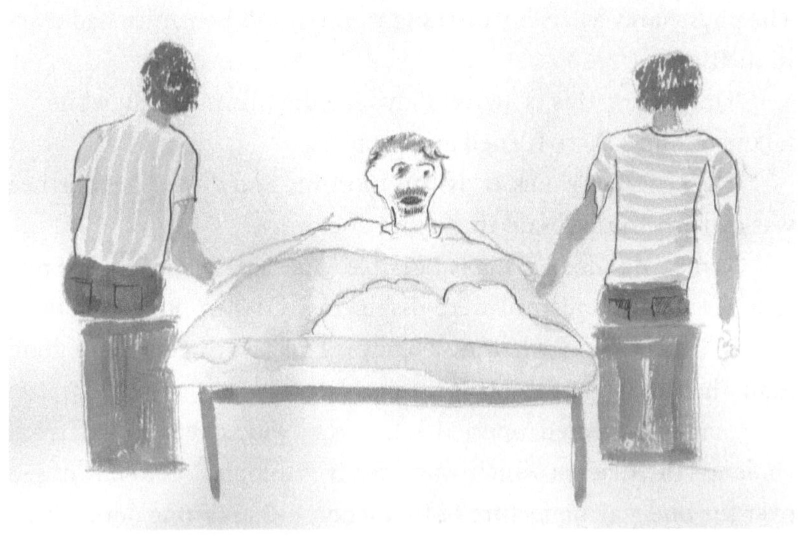

"That is for my house," the driver said as he got back into the vehicle, oblivious of the urgency of getting to Addis.

The two finally reached a new stretch of highway leading up to the tunnel at the halfway point between Addis and Dessie. The span of five miles or so of highway was contracted out to a Spanish engineering company. The macadam was glossy black, and the no-passing lines were sharp and yellow. Several of the drainage ditches were full of large stones and tree branches. The shoulders were already eroding.

As they drove back through the Highlands, Caanen noticed, not for the first time, the great bucolic beauty of the high country—the rolling gait of the camels, the trotting of the donkeys, and the backdrop of multicolored patches of crops on the mountainsides. North of Debre Berhan, the travelers suddenly came upon men saddled and riding horses alongside the road. No more camels were seen.

Caanen reached Harar the following morning and shortly thereafter arrived at the hospital. He was met by Zirro and Benjamin and the young physician with whom he had spoken to on the phone. The physician was visibly distraught. Zirro and Benjamin had tears in their eyes.

"Dr. Robert, this is awful. Floyd, he die this morning while we talked to him." Zirro turned away sobbing.

"He went into shock early this morning and died. The diarrhea was overwhelming," said the young doctor.

Caanen nodded. "This is horrible," he said. Seeing the sorrow that Zirro and Benjamin were displaying, Caanen hugged both of them. "I don't know what to say, boys. This is a tragedy for a good man, the two of you, and this country."

Caanen reflected upon the fact that Floyd likely died from cholera—the disease which was "not in Ethiopia." Caanen mused over the one glaring feature of living here—that is, one never knew what was going on in the world around you, and there were precious few ways to find out. Caanen thought once again of *Death in Venice*. Poor Aschenbach died of a disease that was only bruited about, never openly named.

TIME TO LEAVE

Caanen grabbed his cell phone, which was ringing.

"Yes?"

"That's awful about Floyd. Can we do anything? Maybe it would be best for you to come to Addis. We'll put you up at the Hilton and prepare a return flight," said Evers.

"I'll be there in a day. I'm taking Floyd's body to the airport," said Caanen.

Zirro and Benjamin helped Caanen secure a taxi to take Floyd's body to Addis Ababa.

Caanen left the Bole airport after dropping off Floyd's body. The taxi was elaborately decorated with thick leather pads and fringes over the dashboard. Plastic fruit hung from the rearview mirror, and large brass Ethiopian crosses adorned both visors. The seat was padded with ersatz zebra skin. The car crawled up the steep incline of Menelik II Boulevard. Eventually, the driver, a heavyset man in his fifties, shifted into second gear as he turned into the Hilton compound. The guard waved him forward. Caanen gave the driver a generous tip.

Caanen walked under the long, covered arcade in front of the hotel tower and checked in at the reception desk. He glanced at the bar area that looked out over the pool and the lush vegetation covering the hotel compound. Several women in evening dresses and men in sport suits enjoyed drinks and cigars. He entered the restaurant and was seated by a handsome Ethiopian receptionist wearing a yellow silk *shamma.*

"Can I help you, sir?" said the waitress dressed in black slacks and a white blouse.

All of the hotel employees were Ethiopian and spoke perfect English.

This was the first meal he had looked forward to in months. He waited with a twinge of anticipation. The food preparation was meticulous and attractive. After finishing the meal, he walked downstairs to the pool level where there were shops. He entered the bookstore. Beside the usual sumptuous coffee table books of photographs of tribes of Ethiopia was a paperback book Caanen picked up and thumbed through. The book was titled *Lords of Poverty* and had as its main theme the corrupting process that financial aid to third-world countries engendered. Indeed, the last chapter was titled "Aid Is Not Help." Caanen placed the book back on the rack and walked to his room.

THE DEBRIEFING

Julie had flown back from Bahir Dar. She joined Caanen poolside, and they waited for Evers to arrive for a debriefing conference.

Julie was describing the lack of infection control in the hospital at Bahir Dar. She had spent several successful months making friends with the nurses at the hospital and implementing an awareness of HIV in the hospital setting. Like Dessie, the recent emphasis was on getting patients on medications, and little effort was made to educate the patients about their disease. She looked happy, her raven-black hair drawn back into a ponytail.

"I hope he's not going to lecture like he did before. I can't take it," she said to Caanen, dropping her rhinestone-studded spectacles onto her bodice. "I want to spend my time buying some gifts to take home, not waste time with this guy who doesn't listen to us. This organization is run by nonmedical people. Imagine if the military were run by the bureaucrats."

"Well, let's stay civil at this meeting."

"I will! I want to get on with one of these NGOs and come back here. There's a lot I could help with, but I can't stand being interfered with every week or so."

"I feel the same way you do," Caanen said. "I was glad to work in Dessie. I'm sorry the Dutton Foundation doesn't listen to our advice."

"I figure if they can pay me somewhere near what I earn now, by living here I can actually save money. Besides, I have done all I want to do back home."

Caanen listened to Julie speak about her hospital in Bahir Dar, which happened to be a major tourist stop. Julie had lived in a first-rate hotel surrounded by palm trees on the edge of Lake Tana. She told Caanen about one of her fellow lodgers, an older man in his sixties with no obvious source of money who drank heavily, womanized, swore prolifically, and met in secret with Ethiopians on a daily basis.

"Somehow, I believe that guy actually works for the Dutton Foundation. Maybe he's the fella making policy for Ethiopia."

"I doubt that," said Caanen. "Here is Evers."

"How're you doing, Julie? Dr. Caanen?" Evers pulled up a lawn chair. The waitress came up to him. "Why don't we all have a macchiato?" he said.

Caanen and Julie agreed.

"Well, I'll tell you, we never expected anything like what happened to Floyd. Of course, he was on vacation when all this happened, but still, this makes the government anxious,' Evers said. He had slipped easily into his informal tone of conversation.

Caanen could see Julie out of the corner of his eye and saw she was uncomfortably shifting in her seat.

"I would like each of you to write up an appraisal of your stay. Put in the good and the bad. As you are both aware, our organization is going to provide children with antiretroviral drugs in the hopes of saving this nation," said Evers. He was dressed in gray slacks and a blue blazer over a patterned cream-colored shirt.

"But this whole place is going to come apart if you do it in this fashion, Peter. Can't Dutton understand the concept? The children need their parents. The pregnant mothers need the drugs at delivery," said Julie.

"Look!" said Evers, rising from his chair. "I don't want to cover all of this again. Please give me your comments by email." He walked toward the poolside bar.

Zeleka passed him as she made her way to Julie and Caanen.

Caanen made the introductions of the two women.

"I remember you from Mount Entoto," said Julie.

"Yes, I was there. Wasn't I, Robert?"

Julie glanced at Caanen surreptitiously.

Zeleka was visibly upset when Caanen told Julie about Floyd's death.

The three continued to talk about operational problems for another hour before breaking up. Zeleka left for her room.

Julie looked at Caanen. "You know, she has something for you."

"Is it that obvious? I am hoping that will stop so we can enjoy the last few days."

"Goddamn, that's kind of heartless, Caanen."

"Well, I didn't mean it to sound so harsh. She doesn't have any idea who I am. That is not to say that I am not flattered, I am."

"Well, you're a good man," said Julie.

That evening, Caanen dined alone in the hotel restaurant and looked out over the lush planting of the hotel grounds. The shimmering blue water of the lighted pool was mesmerizing. African and European men stood at the bar puffing on their expensive cigars. Caanen walked to his room and shortly thereafter fell asleep.

FLIMFLAM

Caanen arose early. He was hoping to purchase a guide to the birds of Ethiopia. The young man at the Hilton bookshop was confident that the university bookshop would have a guide. On the way to the university, Caanen decided to stop at the Museum of Natural History. As he approached a traffic circle, he was suddenly aware of a fellow foot traveler to his right.

"Where are you heading?" said a smartly dressed Ethiopian male of twenty who was carrying a book.

"The Natural History Museum."

"That is by the university. Not here."

"The map says it is right over there," Caanen pointed out. "I believe I can see it from here."

"That map is no good. Come with me. I'll show you where it is." The fellow became insistent. "By the way, do you think you can help me with my studies? You can give ten dollars a month, I am sure."

"No! I am going to the museum."

"You're a fool," was the student's Parthian shot.

Caanen entered the museum. The first floor had exhibits mounted on the walls with large panes of glass between the visitors and the mammals and birds indigenous to the country. Caanen became absorbed in trying to identify some of the vultures. A museum employee came up to him.

"Can I help you, sir?" the smiling man said in impeccable English. He was short-statured with a handsome face and remarkably white teeth and appeared to be in his fifties.

Caanen explained what he was interested in. The gentleman happened to be the museum director. He politely guided Caanen to the appropriate display cases. He was extremely knowledgeable about the habitat surrounding Dessie and the birds and animals to be found there. Caanen thanked him for the information and shook his hand.

When he was done at the museum, Caanen started walking up Entoto Road toward the university. He saw the young man who had accosted him walking alongside a European couple and gesturing toward the Natural History Museum. Caanen stealthily crossed over to the other side of the road. He seated himself in the café where he had first met Mr. Z. Million months ago. He ordered a coffee and pastry and waited. Caanen was hoping Million would somehow miraculously show up, and he could make proper amends for not believing what he had been told on his arrival to Addis Ababa. Mr. Million was nowhere to be seen.

Later, he entered the main gate of the university, which had once been an elaborate palace of Haile Selassie. He left his driver's license with the front gate guard and walked over to the bookstore. The building was formerly the barracks for the palace guard. Caanen went into the basement where a clerk said books could be found. He looked about the room. Labels were taped to the wall denoting each physical and social science. The books below the labels were course offerings for the classes. Only a handful of books were stacked below each label. He found one small paperback publication dealing with rare birds of Ethiopia. It was written for children.

While walking back to the hotel, it began to rain lightly. Caanen took a detour into a small public park housing lions, once the proud possessions of Selassie who was known as the Lion of Judah. The entrance fee was exorbitant, and no cameras were allowed. The reason for checking the cameras was soon evident. Official photographers were everywhere and could be hired for a handsome sum. There were several small rotundas with concrete skirts and old iron railings with flaking paint. One could walk up to the cages and stick a hand or foot in the cage, all of which was demonstrated by the grinning photographers.

"I take your picture," the photographer in the black tattered suit and Panama hat said.

The lions appeared bored and could not be aroused to roar or react to the antics of the photographers. A small, nearby outbuilding housed the cubs. Rain started to fall in earnest. Caanen fled the confines of the park and started the long walk back to the Hilton.

LET'S HAVE A DRINK

Upon returning to the hotel, Caanen was handed a slip of paper by a young woman in a magenta pantsuit with gold piping. "This person call while you away," she said.

Dr. Abebe, the director of the HIV clinic in the leprosarium, had left his number and wanted to meet with Caanen at Blue Top Restaurant that evening. Caanen took a taxi to the restaurant.

Other Anglos were eating at scattered tables. Dr. Abebe was seated in the corner with a heavyset white man with a closely trimmed white beard. Both of the individuals were big men with generous abdomens. They were old acquaintances. Abebe was one of the Dutton Foundation's oldest employees, and his companion, William Foster, had been with a number of NGOs in Africa. He owned a small place in Ngorongoro Crater where he had spent the past few weeks. His wife lived in Santa Fe and occasionally flew over to meet with him.

"Abebe, you've got to find me a job with Dutton soon so I'll have something to do," said Foster. Foster was a start-up expert for medical clinics, familiar with all of the complexities and requirements of running a clinic in a resource-poor country.

Abebe thought a manager's position would open soon in Lalibela. "We need to get that clinic off the ground," said Abebe.

Abebe thanked Caanen for his service and informed him that he was welcome back anytime if he could spare the time. No mention was made of Evers's assessment of Caanen.

The following morning, Caanen and Julie shared a taxi to the airport. They were both eager to return home.

BACK HOME

Caanen arrived back in the United States without incident. His travel time was spent staring out the window at the clouds, sea, and sky. He immediately started back to work in his HIV clinic, spending an inordinate amount of time solving small problems for patients, all of whom, if they desired, would live to old age.

He worked carefully on a manuscript describing the activities of the clinic in Dessie, pointing out the dedication of the workers and Floyd's death from cholera. Caanen sent a copy of the manuscript to Evers for his comments. He also sent a copy of the current edition of the *Merck Manual* for Mulugeta.

Within two days, Caanen received an email from Evers. It read, in part: "Under no circumstances will you go forward with this paper. It is overly negative and more than likely to be misunderstood."

Caanen was abashed. He decided the best course was to go ahead and publish the paper, because it might influence neighboring countries to think about their approach to HIV and provide a testimonial to Floyd's commitment to Ethiopia. Floyd may have been indiscreet with the young men, but he was a compassionate and generous man who took a personal approach to every patient.

Caanen often reflected upon his experience in Ethiopia. It was true that much good was being accomplished by the Foundation placing patients on antiretroviral medications. A steady pipeline of drugs would save many lives. There was no denying, however, the corrupting presence of all the aid agencies. They delivered a product to the country, but one wondered, would the lasting effect for the country be the corruption of all of the people involved"

Perhaps the most poignant memory was a headline that caught Canaan's attention while looking at BBC online: "Dateline: Addis Ababa, Ethiopia: Lion cubs killed to save money. Due to lack of funds for food, Emperor Haile Selassie's lion cubs have been destroyed."

www.ingramcontent.com/pod-product-compliance
Lightning Source LLC
Chambersburg PA
CBHW030642190726
48286CB00008B/2621